P9-DIY-865

TAKEN!

"Jane!"

For a moment, all Buzz could hear was his own heavy breathing. Then, a soft rustling sound. It came from the brush, deeper in the jungle. As he looked around, he saw a small group, moving almost silently through the woods. They were *kids*, he realized, not much bigger than Jane herself. And even though he couldn't see his little sister, he knew they had her. There was no other explanation.

Buzz clamped a hand over his own mouth to keep from shouting out.

STRANDED

SHADOW ISLAND

BOOK 1: FORBIDDEN PASSAGE

JEFF PROBST

and CHRIS TEBBETTS

PUFFIN BOOKS
An Imprint of Penguin Group (USA)

PUFFIN BOOKS
Published by the Penguin Group
Penguin Group (USA) LLC
345 Hudson Street
New York, New York 10014

USA / Canada / UK / Ireland / Australia / New Zealand / India / South Africa / China
penguin.com
A Penguin Random House Company

First published in the United States of America by Puffin Books,
an imprint of Penguin Young Readers Group, 2014

Copyright © 2014 by Jeff Probst

Penguin supports copyright. Copyright fuels creativity, encourages diverse
voices, promotes free speech, and creates a vibrant culture. Thank you for
buying an authorized edition of this book and for complying with copyright
laws by not reproducing, scanning, or distributing any part of it in any
form without permission. You are supporting writers and allowing
Penguin to continue to publish books for every reader.

CIP Data is available

Puffin Books ISBN: 978-0-14-751388-5

Printed in the United States of America

1 3 5 7 9 10 8 6 4 2

This is a work of fiction. Names, characters, places, and incidents either
are the product of the author's imagination or are used fictitiously,
and any resemblance to actual persons, living or dead, businesses,
companies, events, or locales is entirely coincidental.

I am one of the luckiest guys in the world. I have two of the *most amazing kids on the planet,* and they bestow the greatest honor on me every day—simply by calling me Dad. Without them and my wife, Lisa, *Stranded* would not exist. So *Stranded* is always dedicated to them.

And during the course of writing this book I met a couple of other *suuuper* cool kids who gave me so much inspiration and made me smile so many times that there was no doubt I would dedicate this book to them, too!

CJ and Logan—through your courage, you reminded me to always keep my chin up. I'm glad we're friends.

Okay readers, hang tight. *Shadow Island* is a whole 'nother world. Remember, "The adventure you're ready for is the one you get!"

—JP

With thanks to the Londonderries:
Jan Donley, Barbara Gregorich, Vicki Hayes,
Ruth Horowitz, and Joe Nusbaum

—CT

FORBIDDEN PASSAGE

CHAPTER 1

Carter Benson felt a horrible sense of déjà vu as he stood on the edge of the green and shadowy jungle. He was drenched, out of breath, and already starting to shiver.

How could this be happening *again*?

As he waited for Buzz, Vanessa, and Jane to catch up, he scanned the area for any clues about where they'd just landed. But something else caught his eye.

There, on a rocky point at the far end of the beach, was a girl. Dressed in dried grass, braided leaves, and some kind of leather or skin tunic, she looked unlike anyone Carter had ever seen before. As she stared back, he froze right to his spot. So much had happened in the past twelve hours, his brain didn't seem to know what to make of it. Or of her.

Then again, everything that had happened in the last two weeks would have seemed impossible . . . two weeks ago. How they'd survived a shipwreck and thirteen days on a deserted South Pacific island, Carter wasn't even sure anymore. But at least they'd thought it was over.

It wasn't over.

"Carter?" Nine-year-old Jane came up alongside him. Buzz was there now, too. He and Carter were both eleven, but Carter always got everywhere first.

"HEY!" he shouted out to the girl.

"What is it?" asked their older sister Vanessa, the last to join the group.

Carter turned to all three of his siblings. "There's someone—a girl—right there! Look!"

"Where?" Vanessa asked.

"Right there!"

Shouts were coming out of the woods now. Several of them, from different directions.

"What's that?" Buzz asked. He and the girls turned toward the noise, but Carter kept his eyes on the girl.

She'd crouched down now, nearly out of sight. Before Carter could make any sense of it, she checked once over her shoulder, then stood up, quickly stepped to the edge of the point, and dove. A moment later, she'd disappeared beneath the choppy surface of the water.

Carter ran without thinking. He dug his feet into the sand, sprinting for the shore as fast as he could get there.

"Carter, stop!" Vanessa yelled after him. "We can't split up!"

"What are you doing?!" Jane screamed.

If there had been time, his answer might have been, *I don't know.* Or maybe more like, *Following my gut.* Out here in the wild, hesitation was not their friend. Sometimes you had to take chances just to survive.

And maybe this girl could help them.

* * *

Jane raced along the beach after Carter. Buzz and Vanessa were right behind.

So much had happened in the last two weeks, but Carter was still the same. Once he made up his mind about something, there was no stopping him. Already he had reached the water's edge near the rocks and was sprinting right into the ocean. He never even looked back.

"What about the dinghy?" Buzz called as they ran.

"It's tied off, right?" Vanessa said.

"Yeah, but—"

"Just come on!"

Vanessa was right. The boat was important, but not as important as sticking together. When Jane looked back, she could see the little yellow dinghy where Carter had secured it to a giant piece of driftwood on the dry sand. It would be fine there in the meantime.

And maybe Carter was right, too. There were people on this island—the shouts from the jungle, the girl Carter had seen. Maybe this was exactly the help they needed to survive, possibly even to find their parents, and to be rescued. All over again.

It was never supposed to happen like this. Not in a million years. The dinghy itself had been part of the last rescue. It came with the small airplane that had found them on a deserted rocky atoll Jane had dubbed "Nowhere Island." After thirteen days of struggling for food, water, and shelter in that place, they'd been *this close* to going home again.

Instead, the nightmare had continued. A relentless current had swept them and the boat away from Nowhere Island, away from their parents, and away from any chance of rescue . . . to here.

Wherever *here* was.

———

"Carter, please!" Vanessa screamed, but it was no good. He swam away from them, heading around the rocky point with no sign of slowing down.

It was beyond frustrating. Her younger brother was made of guts and stubbornness, but at thirteen, Vanessa was the oldest. That meant it was her responsibility to keep everyone together. No matter what.

"I'm going to kill him!" Vanessa said. "Seriously. How could he just run like that?"

Her eyes were on the shoreline now, searching for some way to cut him off. Should they climb up onto the rocky point? Head straight into the ocean?

The beach had seemed clear enough a moment ago, but with the next step, Vanessa felt the ground shift. Her foot seemed to slip right through the sand. There was a crackle of dead wood, a splitting sound, and then nothing at all beneath her.

The fall barely even registered—not until she hit the bottom of a sandy pit with a jarring thud. Small sticks and a shower of dirt clods rained over her head.

Her mind scrambled, trying to make sense of what had just happened. Was she hurt? Could she stand up?

"Vanessa!"

Jane's and Buzz's heads both appeared up around the top edge of the pit. They lay on their stomachs reaching for her, but she was too far down. They'd never be able to get to her. Not on their own.

"Can you get out?" Buzz asked.

Vanessa stood slowly, testing her legs to make sure she hadn't sprained anything. She tried jumping—

once, twice, three times—but it was no good. A long night of drifting in the dinghy had left her legs wobbly. Even with six years of gymnastics, she couldn't find the spring she needed. The pit was too deep, its walls too far apart to shimmy up. The sides only cascaded with loose dirt and sand when she tried.

"Why is this hole even here?" Jane asked in a shaky voice.

"I don't know!" Vanessa answered. The possibilities were too scary to think about, and they didn't have time to spare. "Just go look for a vine!"

If there was one thing they had going for them, it was that they knew something about the jungle. Maybe not *this* jungle, but there would be vines, anyway. Just like on Nowhere Island.

"Hurry!" she said.

Vanessa could hear the panic in her own voice. She didn't want to scare Buzz or Jane, but the looks on their faces said everything. They were already terrified.

"What if—" Buzz started to say.

"Just *go*!" Vanessa yelled. "And stay together!"

Buzz headed into the woods with Jane, running as fast as he could.

Before all of this, "adventure" had meant something he did on the couch with a game controller in his hand. But not anymore. Now the jungle was a familiar mix of humidity, swarming mosquitoes, and the sound of a million other bugs and birds.

His eyes had grown keen on Nowhere Island, too. Within a moment of scanning, he spotted bamboo, firewood, and the kind of long ropy vines he'd been hoping to find. They hung in a thick cluster just past the tree line.

"What was that?" Jane asked suddenly.

Buzz whirled around. "What was *what*?"

"I thought I heard something moving around," Jane said.

The shouting from the woods had gone quiet now. Buzz wasn't even sure which was scarier—the shouting or the silence. Not that it mattered. Nothing mattered more than getting Vanessa out of that pit and finding Carter.

"Let's just get this done and get out of here," he said. He wiped his sweaty hands on his tattered shorts. Then he took hold of a low-hanging vine and started to pull.

"Buzz?" Jane said.

"Help me!" he said, putting all of his weight on the vine to free it from the branches overhead. As he did, the sunlight through the canopy made him squint. He thought he saw a shadow moving up there, but it was hard to tell.

"One, two, *three!*" he said, and heaved again. The vine snapped, and Buzz fell back, rolling into the brush.

"Jane, help me!" he said again, with a rush of angry impatience. "Give me a hand!"

But Jane didn't answer.

"Jane?" he said. Buzz scrambled onto his knees and spun around, but she wasn't there. She was just . . . gone.

"Jane!"

For a moment, all Buzz could hear was his own heavy breathing. Then, a soft rustling sound. It came from the brush, deeper in the jungle. As he looked around, he saw a small group, moving almost silently through the woods. They were *kids,* he realized, not much bigger than Jane herself. And even though he couldn't see his little sister, he knew they had her. There was no other explanation.

Buzz clamped a hand over his own mouth to keep from shouting out. That wouldn't help. But neither would losing track of Jane.

Pulse pounding in his ears, he kept to a low crouch. His eyes locked onto the group as they moved farther into the jungle's shadows. Then, stepping lightly, he started following from a distance and, at the same time, tried to figure out what in the world he was supposed to do next.

CHAPTER 2

"**B**UZZ! JANE!" Vanessa screamed for what felt like the hundredth time. Where were they?

Everything had changed so fast. How had they even gotten into this mess?

It was a question she knew the answer to, but that didn't make it easy to accept.

Was it really just a day ago that the rescue plane carrying their parents had landed off the shore of Nowhere Island? Yes, it was. It had felt like some kind of miracle at the time, and the happiest moment of Vanessa's life.

But their luck hadn't lasted long. The rescue plane

itself was too small to carry everyone. None of the family wanted to split up after everything they'd been through, so all six had agreed to wait on Nowhere Island while the crew went for a larger chopper.

Buzz, Vanessa, Carter, Jane, and their parents had spent the rest of the day there together. The plane had left behind plenty of provisions, but it was Vanessa who had come up with the idea of catching fish for dinner. They were going to show Mom and Dad how they'd survived for those thirteen days alone on the island.

"Don't go too far," Beth Benson had said as the kids had climbed into the yellow rescue dinghy.

"No problem," Vanessa had told them. "We'll be back on shore with dinner in half an hour."

But none of them had anticipated how easily the little boat would move through the water. Or how strong the currents could be, as soon as they'd paddled to the far side of their usual fishing reef. Together, it had all spelled disaster.

Vanessa remembered a lot of screaming when the current had taken hold. She'd yelled at Buzz and Carter to paddle back, but the tide had held them in its grip.

Mom and Dad had screamed, too. They'd both dived in and swam, but not as fast as the dinghy had left the island behind. With a shocking kind of speed, it had swept the kids away from the shore and out to sea.

All four of them had struggled against the current, paddling with the oars and their hands until they'd finally dropped into the bottom of the boat, exhausted and unable even to think about what would come next.

Now, all of it ran through Vanessa's mind like the replay of a terrible dream. She'd gone over it a hundred times in the course of the night. There was no way to imagine how they could have avoided this, short of staying on land in the first place. Which they should have done, because here they were, stranded all over again. Or maybe even worse.

Shouts from the distance pulled Vanessa out of her thoughts. She heard voices coming closer, but not those of her siblings.

On instinct, she crouched down. There was nothing else she could do. She was trapped.

A moment later, a scrubby length of vine tumbled into the pit. Vanessa's breath caught in her throat.

Who was at the other end of that vine? What was going on?

"Ekka-ka!" a voice said overhead.

When she looked up, she saw half a dozen faces—all strangers.

"Chafa-ka!" said the same voice. It belonged to a girl about Vanessa's age, maybe thirteen or fourteen.

The girl motioned for Vanessa to climb. Whether or not these people could be trusted, it was impossible to say. But staying in the pit was no option. And one way or another, she had to find Buzz, Jane, and Carter.

With trembling hands, Vanessa took hold of the vine and started to climb. Almost right away, the whole thing jerked in her grip. She felt herself dragged up and out, until she was on the beach again, staring into the strangers' faces. The surf pounded in the distance while the kids chattered around her in whatever language they spoke.

"Please!" she said, trying not to cry. "I have to find my brothers, and my sister! Does anyone speak English?"

No one answered. Their smiles seemed friendly

enough, but there was no way to know what to expect next. All she could imagine were the dozen awful things that might have happened to the others by now.

One of the girls took Vanessa's arm. She motioned toward the woods that ran in a line along the top of the beach. The landscape there changed dramatically, from bright sunny seashore to shadowy jungle within a few feet. Given the urgency in the others' voices, and the way they kept gesturing toward the woods, it seemed as if they wanted Vanessa off the beach.

She looked around quickly, aching for some sign of Jane, Buzz, or Carter. But there was nothing to see.

Several of the strangers were moving now, deeper into the woods. Some of them scrambled up into the trees and began traveling off the ground. Half a dozen of them moved from tree to tree overhead, but not like monkeys. More like . . . what was it called? *Parkour*. Vanessa remembered a kid on the playground showing her how he could do a backflip off the side of a wall, leap over to the top of the slide, do another backflip, and then land on his feet. All in one move.

These kids were doing much the same thing, but twenty feet up. Vanessa watched, stunned, as a girl leaped from the branch of one tree to the trunk of another, sprang off that, and flew past one of the boys in midleap, as both of them landed on adjacent limbs. Neither of them seemed even to look for the next landing spot as they moved on, deeper and deeper into the jungle. It was as though they'd been flying through these trees all their lives—which they probably had.

"Please!" she tried again, to the others still on the ground. Speaking in English wasn't going to help, but she couldn't stop the words tumbling out of her. "Where are the others? The ones I came with?"

Their only answer was to keep pointing, and keep moving into the woods. With any luck, they were headed the same way that Buzz and Jane had gone—and hopefully Carter, too.

If not, Vanessa thought, she was going to have to make a break for it.

Somehow.

Carter's hand ached with every stroke through the water. He'd cut it badly on Nowhere Island, diving for supplies from their wrecked and sunken sailboat. The infection that followed had only just begun to heal, after medical treatment from the rescue crew. But he still couldn't swim as fast as he wanted.

Salt water stung his eyes as he looked around. There was no sign of the girl. How far could she have gotten already?

Continuing around the point, he was careful not to swim too close to the shoreline. It was a tough balance. If he wasn't careful, the waves here could wash him right into the rocks. If he went out too far, he'd lose precious time.

Finally, he spotted her. She was swimming through the clear Pacific, headed back to the beach on the far side of the point.

"Wait!" he shouted, but it came out as a garble in the water. The only thing to do was keep swimming until he caught up to her. Still, his own breath was drawing short, while the girl hadn't shown any signs of slowing down.

Back at home, he never would have worn out this quickly. His mom even called him Tank sometimes, because he never stopped moving. But the days on Nowhere Island had taken their toll.

Before he could get any farther, someone dove into the water next to him. In the white stream of bubbles that followed, he caught only a glimpse of whoever it was. *Vanessa,* he thought. *Or maybe Buzz, or Jane.*

But it wasn't. With a second splash, another body fell right on top of him. Then another. He sank under their weight as they grabbed on. Someone had him now, with two strong arms squeezing him around the chest. Hard. The air from his lungs rushed out in a stream of bubbles.

Carter struggled and twisted in the water, trying to get an arm free—or a fist. But it was no good. Whoever this was had caught him completely by surprise. There were at least three of them, and as far he could tell, they were all stronger than he'd ever be.

As he sank deeper, unable to do anything to stop himself, it hit Carter with a horrible certainty. This was a contest he couldn't win.

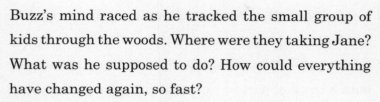

Buzz's mind raced as he tracked the small group of kids through the woods. Where were they taking Jane? What was he supposed to do? How could everything have changed again, so fast?

He still couldn't see his sister, but he could hear the muted sound of her calling for him, somewhere inside the tight cluster that kept her moving along. Her voice alone struck a chord in his heart—a terrified feeling.

As for Vanessa and Carter, who knew where they were by now? If he ran back to the pit and found Vanessa gone, then he'd be completely on his own. At least he could keep track of Jane.

He kept his distance for the time being. The other kids weren't being rough with her, but they were definitely on the move.

They seemed to be a tribe of some kind. Their language was strange to Buzz's ears, and the way they were dressed—leather skins, woven grass or straw tunics, and jewelry made from what looked like shells and colored beads—all seemed "native," if that was the right word. It looked as though everything these kids had could have been found on the island. There were no T-shirts, no sneakers, nothing that looked as if it had come from a store.

Soon, they fell onto a path. It was clearly man-made, with a track of packed earth cutting through the dense foliage. Now they traveled more quickly, but it was also easier for Buzz to keep his footfalls quiet. He kept the group in sight, still not sure what to do, or what to expect.

As they continued deeper into the woods, it seemed to become less wild instead of more. Buzz tiptoed past a fenced pen, with chickens and two boars sleeping in the shade. It all looked well maintained. These boars were nothing like the ferocious, squealing creatures he and his siblings had encountered on Nowhere Island. Even now, the memory of those high-pitched animal screams put a shiver down Buzz's back, right along with the sweat.

Farther on, they approached what looked like a village in the middle of the woods. It was arranged in a wide-open circle around a cleared dirt yard, maybe a hundred feet across. The trees on the perimeter were enormous, with exposed roots that grew out of the ground like ten- and twenty-foot-high tangles of rope. Most of the huts Buzz could see were nestled right into the root systems themselves. It was unlike anything he'd ever encountered, on TV or otherwise.

With his back pressed to the trunk of a gnarled palm, he stayed low, watching from a distance. Jane seemed okay for the moment. The kids who had brought her here were smiling and laughing.

And then Jane's face lit up in a smile, too, just before Vanessa's voice came from somewhere nearby.

"JANE!" Vanessa yelled.

"NESSA!"

The two of them ran to each other and hugged, while the other kids continued to gather around.

"Please," Vanessa said, "can you help us?"

"Does anybody speak English?" Jane asked.

Buzz took a deep breath and stuck to his hiding place. Did it make more sense to run to his sisters now? Or to wait and see what happened?

He didn't know . . . he didn't know. And in a way, that was the worst part.

CHAPTER 3

Carter stumbled into the village, pushed along by the three older boys from the water.

"Carter! There you are!" Jane shouted. She and Vanessa ran to meet him in the middle and threw their arms around him.

"Have you seen Buzz?" Vanessa asked.

"No," Carter said.

"Neither have we," Jane told him. "I don't know what to do."

"How's your hand?" Vanessa asked.

Carter hadn't even noticed he'd lost the bandage somewhere. The cut along his palm was still closed—

no bleeding, but it ached when he flexed it. Even so, the hand was the least of his worries right now.

"Did anyone hurt you guys?" Carter asked.

"We're okay," Jane answered. "So far, they're being nice."

"Not all of them," Carter said. He glared at the three who had brought him here, though he was trembling on the inside. They'd ambushed him in the water, dragged him to the bottom, and then pulled him across the sandy ocean floor to emerge on the beach, gasping for air. It had been a relief to realize they weren't trying to drown him. But the relief hadn't lasted long.

From there, the boys had marched him back through the woods, prodding him forward with long sticks. Now that they'd arrived, they backed off and stood around a small fire at the edge of the village, grinning at him as if he was some kind of prize.

Carter looked away from them and scanned the woods. Was Buzz still out there? Had he been taken somewhere else?

"What are we supposed to do?" Jane asked, just as a tiny movement caught Carter's eye. At the edge of the village, Buzz was there. He watched with wide eyes from behind a low screen of bushes while Carter stared back, trying to figure out what to do.

"Don't look now," he muttered to his sisters, "but I just spotted Buzz."

"*What?*" Jane said, almost turning her head. Carter pulled her in tight to keep her from glancing around. Vanessa was steadier, and looked right into Carter's eyes instead.

"Where is he?" she asked low.

"Behind you, about thirty feet away," Carter said.

The whole time, Buzz had been perfectly still in his hiding spot. Now, he held up a thick piece of bamboo, grasped in both hands like a bat, or a weapon.

Before they'd left home in Chicago, Buzz had been the family couch potato. He had some serious gaming skills, but that was about it. Carter was the jock of the family. Jane was the brain. And Vanessa was just a bossy teenager. Or at least, that's how Carter had always thought of it, back when stuff like that had mattered.

Up until two months ago, they hadn't even been brothers and sisters. Not until Vanessa and Buzz's dad had married Carter and Jane's mom. It was as if Carter and his new siblings had had zero in common until all of this craziness had begun. It wasn't exactly the bonding experience their parents had imagined when they all set out for a vacation in Hawaii—but that felt like a lifetime ago by now.

With his eyes locked on Buzz's, Carter gave a tiny shake of his head. *Stay put,* he thought.

But Buzz shook his head, too, as if to say, *No way. I can't. I have to help.*

Carter glared back to try to stop him, but it was too late. Buzz was already on his feet. With a heavy rustling from the brush, he came tearing into the middle of the village, brandishing the bamboo and yelling at the top of his lungs.

"AUUUUGHHHHHHH!"

Buzz ran blindly toward his siblings, shouting as he came.

The bamboo he'd found was his only defense. Maybe he could at least create a distraction, and they could run.

"Let them go!" Buzz screamed.

"Buzz, we're okay!" Jane said. "Don't hurt anyone!"

"What?" Buzz looked toward Jane and, at the same moment, felt his own feet cross, or stumble over a root in the ground. Whatever happened, he flew forward and landed hard in the dirt.

Without stopping, he rolled over. Where was the bamboo? Had he lost it?

At that moment, he came face-to-face with a boy about his own age holding the stick he'd just dropped. Heart pounding, Buzz roared again and put his fists up.

But the boy didn't seem to understand the gesture. He only extended his own hand to help Buzz up.

Several others around the village were laughing and shouting again. The boy took a skin pouch on a cord from his shoulder and handed it to Buzz. It was filled with some kind of liquid.

As scared as Buzz felt, the one thing he needed most of all was a drink. Tentatively, he lifted the skin to his cracked, sunburned lips and took a sip. It was exactly what he'd hoped for—cool, fresh water. The boy who had given it to him smiled, then motioned with his hand for Buzz to take all of it if he wanted.

"Fania," he said. Or at least, something that sounded like it to Buzz's ears.

"Water?" Buzz asked him, knowing the boy couldn't understand him any more than he could understand the boy. Still, they both nodded.

"Fania," Buzz said, finally cracking a smile as he drank some more, then handed the skin pouch to Vanessa to drink some and pass around. In the last two weeks, there had been nothing more important to them than water and fire—and nothing that could raise their spirits so quickly.

"Are you okay?" Vanessa asked, pulling him in close. "I thought you were lost."

"What's going on?" Buzz asked.

"We don't know," Carter answered.

"It seemed like they just wanted me off the beach more than anything," Vanessa said.

"Me, too!" Jane said. "Almost like it was a . . . game or something."

"Not for me," Carter said. "Believe me, those guys weren't playing games."

As Buzz looked around, some of the kids stared back with friendly expressions. But others looked more wary, or even hostile—especially the older ones, who were maybe fifteen at the most.

And that wasn't all. "Where are the grown-ups?" Buzz asked.

"I was just thinking the same thing," Vanessa said. The only people in the village were kids. If there were any adults here, or babies for that matter, none of them were anywhere in sight.

This new world was getting stranger by the minute.

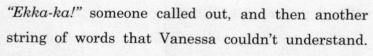

"Ekka-ka!" someone called out, and then another string of words that Vanessa couldn't understand. When she looked around again, she saw several of the younger children coming forward with food.

She almost cried at the sight of it. On Nowhere Island, they'd gone hungry longer than this, but it was a feeling she'd never gotten used to.

There was coconut, yellow fruit of some kind, and even meat, wrapped up in a thick green leaf. It was warm in Vanessa's hand when she took it, and her stomach vetoed any indecision she might have had. The other three seemed to agree. All four siblings dropped to the ground and ate quickly while the village kids watched, laughed, and spoke among themselves.

"Listen," Buzz said, "if they can't help us get rescued, I say we go back and get in the boat. Our best chance of being spotted is on the water, not on land."

Vanessa didn't question him. Ever since they'd gotten stranded on Nowhere Island, Buzz had proven that he knew more about survival than any of them, all from the endless TV he watched at home.

"Okay, but let's wait a little bit," she said. "We still don't know if they can help us or not."

"They're already helping us," Jane said through a mouthful of meat and coconut. "Besides, wouldn't it be better to leave first thing in the morning instead of now?"

Before they could decide anything, one of the older boys shouted from the far side of the village. His voice sounded angry, and when Vanessa looked over, he was pointing at the four of them accusingly.

"That's one of the ones who grabbed me in the water," Carter said through clenched teeth. Carter hadn't told them exactly what had happened out there, but he obviously didn't like this boy.

And from the way the kid was yelling, it seemed as if the feeling was mutual. Or maybe worse.

Another boy walked into the middle of the yard and stood next to Vanessa and her siblings. He shouted something back, pointing from one of them to the next.

The first boy, the angry one, walked out to meet him. Carter started to jump up as he did, but Vanessa yanked him back down.

"Don't even think about it," she said.

"I owe that guy," Carter said. "He practically drowned me."

"Yeah, well, now we're eating their food—so leave it alone!" Vanessa whispered fiercely. They couldn't afford Carter's temper right now. She was ready to wrestle him to the ground herself if she had to.

Meanwhile, the argument between the boys had

spread to the others in the village. There were shouts back and forth from one hut to another, and the two boys at the center were face-to-face, with fists clenched at their sides.

"What's happening?" Jane asked. "What do you think they're saying?"

"It's obviously about us," Vanessa said. Everyone, whether friendly or not, kept looking back their way, pointing and then arguing. "I don't think they all want us here."

"Hang on a second!" Buzz interrupted. He had a faraway look on his face, with his head cocked to the side. "Do you hear that?"

Everyone seemed to pick up on it at the same time. The whole village went still, as if the argument had suddenly been put on pause. And that's when the sound broke through. A low hum was coming from the direction of the water. It was far-off, but distinct.

Vanessa's heart leaped. "Yes!" she said, and grabbed Jane in a hug.

This was what they'd been waiting for since they'd been washed away from Nowhere Island.

It was the sound of a plane.

        ◄————————

Jane could feel the immediate change in the village. It was as if the approaching plane had erased any disagreements, and everyone started working together with a singular purpose. People ran to their fires and kicked sand on them to put them out. Others took to the trees, climbing toward the highest branches overhead.

One boy shimmied up the trunk of a palm at an amazing speed. Halfway up, he let go with both hands, pushed off with his feet, and leaped to the branch of another tree. Then he pulled himself higher and kept on climbing.

Several others had reached the treetops ahead of the boy. Now there were at least a dozen kids up there, moving around. There was some kind of structure, too, Jane realized. Long pieces of bamboo were lashed to the tree trunks, and there was something bound up in a kind of mesh that was made from thin vines.

"What's going on?!" Vanessa shouted. "What are they doing?"

"I don't know!" Jane said. "But we need to keep one of those fires going! Something we can use to make a signal!"

It was impossible to know if Mom and Dad were on that plane. Jane imagined they were, but it didn't even matter. What mattered was getting the plane's attention before it passed by.

Still, the villagers seemed intent on doing just the opposite. The fires had all been extinguished by now. And when Jane looked up again, she couldn't believe what she saw.

As the kids in the trees pulled and adjusted the framework high over their heads, a giant screen of fronds, leaves, and vines had begun to slide into place. Within moments, the whole village was thrown into shadow. Where there had been a circle of sky, now there was a thick camouflage of overlapping green and brown.

"How are we going to be seen?!" Vanessa called.

"They don't WANT to be seen!" Jane said. As for why, there was no time even to think about it.

"We have to get back to the beach!" Buzz said. "We have to signal that plane ourselves. Now!"

In the confusion, everyone seemed to have forgotten about them. And nobody tried to stop them as Jane, Carter, Vanessa, and Buzz turned to sprint out of the village and back toward the beach.

CHAPTER 4

The path through the woods wasn't as easy as Buzz expected.

"Which way?" he asked, as they came to a fork. On the way in, it had seemed like a straight shot. Now, there were turns and divisions none of them had noticed before.

"Just keep moving!" Vanessa said.

Soon, they reached a point where there was no path at all. The jungle grew thicker here, forming a wild barrier between themselves and the beach.

"Can you see the water?" Buzz asked.

"I think so!" Carter said, pushing through. "This

way!" He'd veered on a diagonal, crashing through some low, thick brush. There wasn't any time to make a plan. The only thought now was, *Get to the beach.*

Jane had also disappeared into the brush. Buzz could see the tall snake plants rustling back and forth where she was making her own path. Vanessa was right behind him. And the entire time, the sound of the plane was growing more distant.

With a final push through a brambly thicket that tore at his ankles, Buzz came to the top edge of the beach. The ground changed underfoot, from packed earth to soft sand, and he dug in with each step to get out into the open as fast as possible.

"Do you see the plane?" Carter asked. He was already standing in the sun with his neck craned toward the sky. "Is it there? Do you see it?"

Vanessa and Jane were looking up, too, but Buzz scanned the beach instead.

He looked for the dinghy, but it was nowhere in sight. The spot where they'd left it was just empty sand.

There were no footprints, either. The beach had

been combed clean, as if they'd never been there at all.

"You guys—LOOK!" Buzz said.

Vanessa whirled around. "Where's the boat?" she asked.

"It must have washed away," Carter said.

"I don't think so," Buzz answered. The driftwood they'd tethered it to was still there on dry sand. Only the boat was missing.

"It doesn't matter," Carter said. "Here! We can use this!" He pounced on a fallen tree and started pushing it toward the water. It wasn't a lifeboat, or even a raft, but it was something.

"He's right!" Jane said. "We just have to get out there so they can see us!"

Buzz reached under the log with the others and heaved his end off the ground. There was no time to talk about their dinghy, or the sand that now appeared strangely undisturbed. Besides, there was no need. With any luck, they'd be off this island and headed away from here sooner rather than later.

Hopefully, he'd never even have to find out what

that combed-clean beach and missing boat meant. Because they sure didn't feel like *good* things.

Carter was first in the water. Even with the rush, it felt good to cool his skin after the hard run through the jungle and the push to get their makeshift float into the ocean.

"Kick!" Carter yelled as they all grabbed on. "Everyone facing the horizon!"

It was the only way they were going to get themselves out far enough to be seen by a passing plane.

"How far do you think we have to go?" Jane asked. She was on Carter's right, blinking away the salt water that washed in their faces. Her arms curved like two big claws over top of the log, holding tight.

Carter looked out again. The heaviest surf was well off the shore. He could see it straight ahead where the ocean water turned from a light sky blue to a dark, aqua green. He didn't want to think about how far it might be to open water. Or what they'd have to do to get there. The current had already begun to work against them, and the log tossed in the first low swells.

"Just kick as hard as you can!" he called.

With the next wave, all four of them rose sharply up and back down again with the log. Carter felt a familiar swoop in his stomach—the same kind he'd felt all night long as they blew across the ocean in the dinghy.

He looked over his shoulder. At least fifty yards of water now stretched between them and the beach. But the ocean wasn't getting any calmer in this direction. If they wanted to make it to open water, they were going to have to power through the white wall of a surf break, straight ahead.

There was no going around this one. All Carter could do was duck his head, kick as hard as he could—and then try to kick a little bit harder.

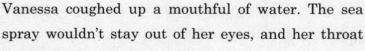

Vanessa coughed up a mouthful of water. The sea spray wouldn't stay out of her eyes, and her throat was raw from swallowing salt.

Overhead, the plane was nowhere in sight. She

couldn't hear it anymore, either. Not over the sound of the ocean. All she could do was hope it would circle back around, and that the four of them would show up against the water's surface when it did.

As soon as they got past the heaviest surf, they could stop kicking so hard. But not now. Not yet. Vanessa ignored the cramps in her feet and calves and kept on kicking.

"We're getting there!" she shouted to the others. "Just keep—"

Her words were cut off by a wave breaking over their heads. Vanessa felt her arms dragged off the log, and she flipped, sucked backward by the pull of the water.

As she came upright, the rolling surf had filled the ocean around her with foam and bubbles, too dense to see through. She felt someone brush against her and grabbed on.

"Vanessa!" It was Jane's voice. Jane was a better swimmer than Buzz, and at least as good in the water as Carter. She pointed over Vanessa's shoulder, where both of their brothers were still holding on to the log, maybe twenty feet away. They were kicking and trying to get back to the girls, even as another wave rose and crested behind them.

"LOOK OUT!" Vanessa shouted, but there was nothing they could do. There was the sound of it first, then a cascade of water burying them in the churning ocean. It all happened too fast, even for a quick breath.

A second time, she came up near Jane, and wrapped an arm around her waist.

"Over here!" Carter yelled. He was in the water now, this time with no log—and no Buzz.

"Hey!" Buzz's voice came from behind. As Vanessa turned, she saw him still clinging to the dead tree. It skimmed across the water, picking up speed on another swell. Before she could get out of the way, the rough bark caught her along the side of the head with a painful, sandpapery scrape that left a ringing in her ear. She reached blindly for Buzz. Her fingers latched onto his arm, but she managed only to drag him off the log as it moved past.

"We can't keep going!" Vanessa yelled.

"What?" Buzz asked, shouting over the waves.

"Come on!" She started swimming toward the beach, not sure how else to tell them what she meant.

"Where's the log?!" Carter yelled. It had disappeared in the confusion. They were all treading water, flapping their arms against the tide.

"Forget the log!" Vanessa said. "This isn't working!" They had to get to shore before the surf took them down for good.

Even stubborn Carter seemed to see that now. It took him a second, and another tumble in a wave, but this time, it washed them all back toward the island.

This place seemed to have them in its grip. And it wasn't letting go.

CHAPTER 5

For the second time that day, Jane stumbled onto the shore of the new island. She dropped to her knees in the wet sand, heaving to catch her breath.

It was clear now that they weren't going to paddle some log into the open water. She was a good swimmer, but none of them were a match for these tides. The ocean itself was enough to keep them prisoner here. And the chances of ever seeing their parents again seemed to be dimming by the minute.

All at once, a shadow darkened the ground around her.

"Qui êtes-vous?" a deep voice said.

Jane spun around and fell back. She looked up at the outline of someone towering over her—then heard her brother nearby.

"Hey! What are you doing?" Carter shouted.

The tall stranger spun in Carter's direction. His face caught the sun, and Jane saw that he was a fully grown-up man. This was the first adult they'd found in this place.

"You speak English," the man said. His heavily accented voice was calm, even as Carter rushed toward them.

"Don't touch my little sister!"

The man caught Carter's wrist and stepped back, quickly letting go again. As he did, Carter lurched right past him and landed on the sand next to Jane. Buzz and Vanessa were just steps away. They knelt close together, looking unsure of what to do next.

"Do not be afraid," the new stranger said. His huge hand enclosed Jane's as he helped her off the ground.

Jane pulled away and moved quickly to stand with Vanessa and Buzz. Carter jumped up, too, fists at his sides.

"Who are you?" Vanessa demanded.

"I am Ani," he said simply.

His clothes were like the others on the island. A tan animal skin was wrapped around his middle, with woven braids of leaves and straw hanging on either side. He was thin, but muscled like an athlete. And he had a large tattoo around his shoulders, in a pattern of rectangles that formed a keyhole shape on his chest.

"You must come with me," he said. "Off the beach."

"We can't! There was a plane!" Vanessa said.

"Yes, I know," he said.

"Our parents might have been up there! Can you help us? Please?" Buzz asked.

"First, you must come with me," the man told them. "Right away."

"You don't understand!" Carter told him.

"I am afraid it is you who do not understand."

Everything happened quickly then. The man strode forward, erasing the distance between them. Jane turned to run, but it was too late. In one fast motion, he'd wrapped an arm around her middle and scooped her off the ground.

The next thing Jane knew, he was running with her toward the woods.

"Carter!" she screamed. "Buzz! Vanessa! Help me!"

"Don't let him get away!" Buzz yelled.

They ran after the stranger—Ani, he'd called himself—but he was far faster than any of them, including Carter. He carried Jane under one arm as though she didn't weigh anything at all. Jane screamed again, and reached for them, squirming to get free. It was a helpless feeling for Buzz, watching the gap between them grow. If this guy made it into the woods, he was going to be even harder to catch, if not impossible.

But then, as the man reached the first line of trees, he stopped. He turned around to face them, gently set Jane down in the shade, and held her by the shoulder until Carter, Vanessa, and Buzz were there.

"What do you think you're doing?" Carter said, snatching Jane away.

"Forgive me. I knew you would have to follow if

I took her," Ani told them. He knelt down then and looked Jane in the eye. "I meant you no harm. I needed only to get you away from the shore."

"What for?" Buzz demanded. He was more angry than scared now. "And where's our boat?"

"Your boat has been taken," Ani said.

"What?" Carter blurted.

"It was not safe to leave it on the beach."

"What do you mean, not safe?" Buzz asked.

"Not safe for *who*?" Vanessa asked.

Ani took his time answering. Everything he told them seemed to be carefully considered.

"The tides are not passable in that direction," he said, pointing toward the horizon. "You would have died trying."

"It's our boat! You didn't have any right to take it!" Vanessa shouted at him.

Ani gave her a stern look. It was the first sign of emotion Buzz had seen on his face.

"You are welcome here," he told them, "but it is not for you to say how the Nukula conduct themselves. You are in *their* home."

"The Nukula?" Jane echoed in a small voice. "I read all about the South Pacific before we ever came here. I've never heard of them."

"That is because they do not want you to have heard of them," Ani said. "The Nukula are a private people."

"Do any of the others speak English?" Jane asked.

"No," he said, offering no further explanation.

"What's this island called?" Jane asked. She always asked a lot of questions when she was nervous. It was a habit Buzz had noticed a long time ago. For Jane, information was security.

"The island has no name," Ani told her. "Not to the Nukula. They have no desire to be known by the outside world. That is why your bright yellow boat had to be removed from the shore."

"Well, where is it now?" Vanessa asked.

"That, I do not know," Ani said, and gestured into the woods. "Come, please. There is much to discuss back at the village."

Buzz felt at a loss for words. On Nowhere Island, the decisions about what to do next were always up to them. Here, it was turning into something even harder. How were they supposed to deal with all of this?

"We're not going anywhere until you tell us what's going on," Carter said. "Are you going to help us get out of here, or not?"

This time, Ani didn't pause. He pushed into the brush, leading the way toward the village.

"That is what I am trying to do," he called back. "Now come. There is no other choice."

CHAPTER 6

The feeling in the pit of Carter's stomach was like a knot and a fist at the same time. He wanted to run— and he wanted to fight. But neither one was going get them anywhere.

It seemed clear they'd been watched from the moment they got here. The yellow dinghy would have been visible for miles off shore as they approached the island. All those kids with their capture games had been waiting for them, hadn't they? And now Ani had been sent to gather them up again.

There was no mistake about who was in control here. The question was, what could Carter, Jane,

Vanessa, and Buzz do about it? The four of them seemed to be numb with new information. There were a million things to say, but they barely spoke all the way up the path and back into the village.

What they found when they got there was a hive of activity.

With the plane gone, the enormous frond net had been pulled away. A circle of empty sky showed overhead once more. Most of the smallest children were gathered near the tops of the trees, playing in the branches.

But the older kids were involved in something else, Carter saw. Some of them were wrestling. He recognized the two-arm grip one of the boys had put on him in the water. Some were using stone hatchets and knives to turn long sticks into spears. And others were rebuilding their small fires. Their friends seemed to be cheering them on, as if even the fire building were a game, or some kind of practice.

Strangest of all, there were now dozens of adults in the village. Where they'd come from, Carter had no idea. But all of their activity stopped as he and his siblings followed Ani into the center of the main dirt yard.

One group of adults in particular seemed to be waiting for Ani. They stood just inside the largest of all the buildings—a longhouse of some kind. Unlike the raised huts, this one sat on the ground. Inside, half of the rough plank floor was raised like a trapdoor. But from where Carter stood, it was impossible to see what lay underneath.

"Stay here," Ani told them, and walked away to speak with the adults.

"What do we do now?" Jane asked, looking around.

"I don't know," Vanessa said. "I guess we wait."

"I don't like waiting," Carter muttered. There wasn't much choice, so he scanned the village instead, looking for any kind of information he could use.

The huts were clustered in some places, and spaced out in others, where the dense jungle showed through. Besides the path they'd just traveled, half a dozen other trails led away from the main yard in all different directions.

The buildings themselves were made from timber and bamboo, with steep thatched roofs. They looked like complete houses compared to the little shelter Carter, Vanessa, Jane, and Buzz had struggled to make on Nowhere Island just a few days earlier.

Coming around full circle, Carter spotted the girl from the beach. She sat in the opening of a tiny hut he hadn't even noticed before, high up in one of the trees. It was the smallest, and easily the sloppiest, of all the buildings in the village, with a patchy roof that didn't look as if it would do much against the rain.

"That's her," Carter whispered to Buzz, and pointed up. "She's the one I saw when we got here."

Mostly, her focus was on the older Nukula kids. She watched them from above, as they made fire, wrestled, and created tools for themselves. It was if she were studying them, or sizing them up, though Carter had no idea why.

The one thing that seemed clear was that this girl was alone. Her hut was barely big enough for a single person to sleep in. And while all the other kids worked in groups, she sat by herself, just watching. Maybe she was even lonely, Carter thought, but it was hard to tell from her stony expression.

Still, he couldn't shake the feeling that she was a possible ally here. A possible friend.

Or, at least, not an enemy.

Jane wanted to memorize everything she saw, and everything she'd learned about this place. Besides wishing to see Mom and Dad again, what she wanted most was her camera, or the paper journal she'd left behind on Nowhere Island. One day this was going to make an amazing story, and she'd be the one to tell it.

Unless, of course, they never got out of here. But that was more than she could stand to think about right now.

Instead, she focused on the people, the clothing, the buildings, the trees—all of it. And she thought about the journal entry she'd write, if only she could.

> This is Jane Benson, reporting for Evans-
> ton Elementary. Today is July twelfth. It's
> been eighteen days since we sailed away

from Hawaii. Fourteen days since the shipwreck on Nowhere Island. And now, Day 1 on the new island. I don't know what's going to happen next, and the truth is, I'm really, really scared. I know Carter, Vanessa, and Buzz are, too, but everyone expects the baby to be afraid. So I'm not going to cry. Not in front of all these people.

Right now, we're in the Nukula village. I've counted 103 people, and 22 huts, built right into the trees. I think these are called banyan trees, but I'll have to look that up—

"What's taking so long?" Buzz said between clenched teeth. "I don't like this."

"Me, neither," Vanessa said, just as Ani finally turned and headed back their way.

"About time," Carter said.

Only Jane stayed silent.

"You have come on an auspicious day," Ani said

as he approached. "For the Nukula, this is the eve of *Raku Nau.*"

Jane squinted up at him. It seemed as if every answer they got only raised more questions.

"What's *Raku Nau?*" she asked.

"In the Nukula language, it means 'journey of the worthy.' It is a test. A passage from youth to adulthood. All Nukula are given one chance to complete *Raku Nau* before their five thousandth day," Ani said.

"Their five thousandth day of what?" Buzz asked.

"It is how age is measured here."

Quickly, Jane's mind turned over the numbers. Three hundred and sixty-five days in a year, times ten, equaled 3,650. That meant she was almost 3,650 days old herself. And then, to get to five thousand days . . .

"That's fourteen years old," she said. "Almost."

Ani raised his eyebrows when he looked at her. "Yes," he said.

"But why are you telling us this?" Vanessa asked.

"Listen to me carefully. You must ask to run *Raku Nau,*" Ani told them. "All of you."

"What? Why?" Vanessa asked.

"*Raku Nau* ends with a ceremony at the far side of the island, on the leeward slopes of *Mayamaka*."

"*Mayamaka?*" Jane asked.

"It means 'Cloud Ridge'," Ani told them.

"But what if—" Buzz started to say before Ani held up a hand to silence him.

"The far shore of the island, beyond *Mayamaka,* is guarded by a small faction of Nukula. The only possible way to reach it is to finish *Raku Nau*. All four of you. Do you understand?"

"No," Buzz said. "What are you even talking about? Why is it guarded?"

"Hang on a second," Jane said. It was coming together like puzzle pieces. Everything Ani had been telling them was for a reason, wasn't it?

"You said before that we couldn't get past the tides on the beach," Jane said, pointing in the direction of the shore where they'd landed with the dinghy. "On *that* beach, right?"

Ani didn't exactly smile, but he gave an encouraging look.

"Beyond Cloud Ridge, and only from there, the tides flow away from the island," he explained.

"Instead of against it," Vanessa said, catching on. She gave Jane an amazed look—the same kind Jane had gotten from her teachers lots of times, when she was the first to come up with the answer to a complicated problem.

"Don't all the tides go in both directions?" Jane said. "In, then out?"

"To a point," Ani said. "But there is only one safe passage from the island. That is why it is guarded."

"So . . . that's the way out of here," Buzz said.

"The momentum there will push you out to sea. You'll seem to be lost, but you'll be visible from above," Ani continued. "If someone is looking for you, they will have a possibility of finding you, away from the island."

"What about our boat?" Vanessa asked.

But Ani shook his head. "I cannot help you with that. I can give you information. What you do with it is up to you."

"We could build a raft," Jane said. "We've done it

before. As long as there's bamboo over there—"

"Do not assume too much, too soon," Ani said. "*Raku Nau* is a difficult journey. Not all who participate will reach the end. Those who are first to finish become tribe leaders, and some of those will one day become elders."

As he said "elders," he indicated the group in the longhouse. Jane noticed that all of them were heavily decorated with beads and tattoos, while other adults wore simple grass dresses or skin wraps, but little more.

"What about everyone else?" she asked.

"Those who do not succeed in *Raku Nau* are considered unworthy of Nukula leadership," Ani explained. "They serve the tribe in lowly functions. They do not participate in decision making for the village."

"You mean, your whole life is decided by the time you're fourteen?" Jane asked. "That's not fair."

"What you see as fair or unfair, the Nukula see as a way of life," Ani said. "There is a need for both leaders and helpers in the tribe."

"Hang on a second," Carter interrupted. "Why should we even trust you, anyway?"

Jane felt embarrassed by Carter's pushy tone, but it *was* a fair question.

Ani nodded. He seemed to think so, too.

"I know what it is to be washed ashore here. You are the first since myself, and that was many years ago," he said.

"And you weren't allowed to leave?" Vanessa asked.

"I did not wish to," Ani answered. "My family was lost in the storm that stranded me here. I was the only one who survived."

"But we *do* have family!" Buzz said. "That's what we've been trying to tell you. Our parents are looking for us."

"Yes," Ani answered simply.

The single word seemed to speak for itself. Jane looked up into his placid face. This man understood them, didn't he? Even if his loyalty was to the Nukula, he'd been through what they'd been through, too.

It wasn't much. *But it was something,* Jane thought. And as all four of them had learned the hard way on

Nowhere Island, sometimes *something* was the most you could hope for.

Vanessa spoke up next, and blurted out an answer.

"We'll do it!" she said. "Tell them we want in. Ask them!"

"What are you talking about?" Buzz said. "We don't even know what this *Raku Nau* thing is."

"It's our only choice. At least there's a chance that way," Vanessa said. It barely mattered what they were saying yes to, because nothing else was even close to acceptable. Whatever *Raku Nau* involved, it had to be better than living on the island indefinitely.

"We still don't know if he's telling the truth," Carter said, glaring at Ani.

It was strange, speaking so openly in front of all these people. But even as Vanessa glanced around, it was clear that nobody understood them any more than she understood the Nukula language.

"I vote yes," she said, looking at her sister and two brothers.

"Me, too," Jane said.

Buzz slowly raised his hand.

"Yeah, okay, fine," Carter said. He pointed a finger at Ani. "But if you do anything to hurt us—"

"Carter, stop!" Vanessa said. Right now there were two possibilities. Either Ani was lying, which she doubted, or he was telling the truth. And either way, they needed him to trust them, just as much as the other way around.

"Please, Ani," she said. "Tell the elders we want to do this."

"It is not only the elders who need to know," he said.

"Who else?" Jane asked.

"Everyone," Ani answered. He turned then and spoke out in a booming voice, addressing the entire village in their own language.

Whatever he told them, Vanessa could see that it stirred a strong reaction. There were shouts of surprise, and sudden conversations cropped up everywhere. The small group of elders began to speak among themselves.

But not for long. A tall woman with a cascade of

beads down the front of her grass tunic turned to face Vanessa, Carter, Jane, and Buzz. When she held up a single palm, the rest of the village grew quiet.

Vanessa held her breath.

"Fah!" the woman said, followed by more of the Nukula language. Even before Ani began to explain, it seemed clear that the woman was saying no.

"I am sorry," Ani told them. "She says it is too soon. You are not known to the Nukula. Not yet. Perhaps next time, once you have earned their trust."

"When is . . . next time?" Jane said.

"Another season. Perhaps another year," Ani said.

Vanessa could barely believe what she was hearing. Another season? *A year?* This couldn't be happening. Her eyes burned with tears.

"Ask again," she told Ani. "Please!"

"They have to give us a chance," Jane said.

"At least that!" Buzz said. All of them of them were on the verge of crying now, but none of the Nukula came near to comfort them. They watched, and listened. And for a long time, it was quiet.

But then another voice broke the silence.

"Ah-ka-ah!" someone yelled from across the yard. Vanessa looked and saw one of the oldest boys, standing with his friends.

"Who is that?" Carter asked Ani.

"Chizo," Ani told him. "Many expect him to be chief of the Nukula one day. But first, he must complete *Raku Nau,* like anyone else."

The way Carter's eyes narrowed, Vanessa knew that Chizo must have been one of the boys who had captured him on the beach.

"What did he say?" Buzz asked.

"He said yes," Ani explained. *"Ah-ka-ah.* He wishes to compete against you."

Slowly, the boy sauntered over to where they stood. Carter stepped in close, but Chizo's eyes were on Vanessa.

It was a look Vanessa had seen before, at gymnastics tournaments and on the soccer field—even in school sometimes—among the most competitive kids. They were the ones who were already thinking about which college they had to get into.

She knew, because she was one of those kids.

Without looking away, the boy spoke again.

"He asks if you're prepared for this," Ani said.

Vanessa kept her eyes up and met Chizo's gaze. *"Ah-ka-ah!"* she said.

Murmurs of what sounded like approval came from around the yard. But not from Chizo. His look was unflinching, with just the hint of a smile.

"What's your problem?" Carter said, but the boy only sneered and walked away. Vanessa expected her brother to follow after him, but for once, he held back. Maybe even Carter could see that he and Chizo wanted the same thing right now—a chance for them to run *Raku Nau.* Even if it was for very different reasons.

Conversation was buzzing all around the village again, mostly among the young. They called out to one another, from hut to hut, tree to tree, and across the round dirt yard.

Then Chizo yelled again, louder than the rest.

"Ah-ka-ah!" he shouted, facing the elders.

As he continued speaking, Ani translated quietly. "He says, 'I am not afraid of these strangers. Let them compete and see true Nukula spirit in us.'"

"*Ah-ka-ah!*" Chizo repeated, and the others took it up as a chant. The village quickly filled with the sound of their voices. All the youngest Nukula were calling for Vanessa, Buzz, Carter, and Jane to be given a chance.

"*Ah-ka-ah! Ah-ka-ah! Ah-ka-ah!*"

Vanessa's insides twisted with a scared, hollow feeling. This was getting more real by the second. Ani looked over his shoulder at the elder council, or whoever they were. They seemed to be the ones who made the final decisions.

"Wait here again," Ani said, and went to speak with them. Vanessa felt Jane press in closer at her side.

"Don't worry," Vanessa told her.

"I'm not worried," Jane said, though it wasn't very convincing. Vanessa was worried, too.

After another long wait, Ani finally came back to where they stood.

"What'd they say?" Buzz asked.

"They do not believe you are capable of taking this on," Ani told them.

"They're wrong!" Carter said.

"But in the spirit of *Raku Nau*," he continued, "the decision will rest with the young. And they are saying they want you to compete. If you wish to do so, you may."

Vanessa took a deep breath. It was the closest thing to good news they were going to get, but it wasn't exactly a lucky break, either. This was far from over.

"So, what happens now?" Jane asked.

Ani turned again and motioned to indicate the hundred or more Nukula staring at them from all over the village.

"You have asked for permission to show them your worthiness," he said. "So—show them that you are worthy."

CHAPTER 7

The journey started before any of them expected.

Somewhere in the middle of the night, Buzz woke up to shouts around the village, and then the light of a large bonfire in the yard.

He and his siblings had been given a small hut to share. It wasn't much, but he'd fallen right to sleep after a day and a half of not sleeping at all. Now, he shook his head, trying to clear the cobwebs. Something was about to happen.

"What's going on?" Carter asked, jerking awake.

"It's starting," Jane said.

"Already?" Vanessa asked. The light from the fire

caught their faces as they all watched, transfixed.

One by one, the participants were descending from their own huts among the trees. No adults came with them. They walked to the middle of the camp and waited, facing out around the fire.

Each of them, Buzz saw, had a painted face in some combination of red, black, and white. Chizo and his two friends wore red on the left side and black on the right. Four others had made large white circles around their eyes, against a field of red. One small group had black and white stripes horizontally from chin to forehead.

The only one with an unpainted face was the girl Carter had first seen on the beach. She seemed to do everything alone around the village. And now, she seemed to be the only one running *Raku Nau* without some kind of teammate.

By the time Ani motioned for them to come forward, Buzz counted twenty-eight other runners around the fire. The four of them would make it thirty-two.

A few of the others looked to be about his and Carter's age. Mostly, the participants were older.

Ani had said that all Nukula were allowed to decide for themselves when to run *Raku Nau,* as long as it happened by their five thousandth day.

Vanessa had figured out that she was 4,850 days old. Jane, on the other hand, was 3,591 days old. She was easily the youngest and smallest to take this on, but there was nothing they could do about that.

It was time to go.

Ani approached them as they moved toward the fire in the middle of the yard. He whispered something in Vanessa's ear and pointed them toward an empty space on the circle.

"Stand here," Buzz heard him say. "Then follow out of the village when the time comes."

Two adults came forward next—one man and one woman—both carrying torches. They slowly circled the group of participants, looking at each one in turn. As they passed Buzz, he forced himself to keep his eyes up. For everything he'd been through—the pitch-black nights on Nowhere Island, the storms that seemed never to end—this was something else entirely. He was as scared as he'd ever been, but all four of them needed to be strong for one another.

Stronger than ever, starting right now.

Vanessa watched carefully as the two elders completed their circle. Once they'd come all the way around, they continued across the yard and out of the village.

The other *Raku Nau* participants fell in behind. There was no speaking. It was a silent procession with the four siblings at the end of the line, along with Ani.

Soon, they stepped onto another path in the woods. This one led in a new direction, deeper into the forest. The path itself was narrow, just wide enough for them all to move single file. But in the light of the torch that Ani carried behind her, Vanessa could see the trees were marked with paint in the same colors as the participants' faces—red, black, and white.

This was the way others had gone before, she guessed. At the start of *Raku Nau*.

Her stomach let up a nervous tremble. It all seemed suddenly insane. What were they getting into? Yes, it meant the possibility of getting off the island, but for all they knew, it also meant risking their lives before it was over.

"What do we need to be ready for?" she asked over her shoulder.

"Everything," Ani answered. "Use your instincts. Do not try to be Nukula, or anything other than who you are. It will not increase your chances of success."

"What *will* increase our chances?" Vanessa asked. Ani seemed to speak in riddles half the time, but he was also their only lifeline. "Please, Ani. Tell me whatever you can."

"There are thirty-two of you now. Only the first sixteen to reach *Mayamaka* will earn the right to wear the *seccu* beyond the ridge and down to the far shore. That is where the finishers' ceremony is held."

"The *seccu*?" Vanessa asked.

"It is a sacred necklace," Ani explained, pointing toward the two elders at the head of the line. Vanessa hadn't noticed before, but she now realized they each wore a leather cord with a purple stone around their necks. She'd seen the same necklace on some of the other adults in the village, but not all.

"Hang on a second," she said. "The first *sixteen*? We have to get there before half of all these people?"

"That is the way of *Raku Nau*," Ani answered. "I told you before that not all who begin will finish. And not all who finish will wear the *seccu*."

Vanessa took a deep but shaky breath. It seemed as if the rules of this thing just kept getting harder and harder.

"Anything else?" she asked, not even sure she wanted an answer.

"It can be easy to get lost on *Raku Nau*," Ani said. "Your best chance is to keep up with the group. But also be careful of them. They will try to slow you down in any way they can. For each one of you who earns the *seccu*, there will be one Nukula who does not."

"Then . . . why did they all want us to compete?" she asked.

"By adding four runners, you have also added two *seccu* to the competition," Ani said.

He fell silent then, but the full meaning of what he'd just said started to become clear. By entering *Raku Nau*, Vanessa realized, they'd actually increased everyone else's chances of success. At least, that's how the other kids probably saw it. Nobody considered them as a threat here. Nobody thought they could actually do this.

And worst of all—she was beginning to think that maybe they were right.

Jane did her crying in the dark. She kept her head down on the trail, letting the tears run silently while she had the chance. And she put more words down in her imaginary journal as they all proceeded silently through the woods.

Dear Mom and Dad,

I've decided to call this place Shadow Island, because I feel like that's where we are—in a shadow, where nobody can see us. It's not that I'm afraid you'll never find this place. Mostly, I'm afraid that you already did, and that you moved on because we were stuck down here, out of sight.

I know you're out there somewhere. You haven't left the South Pacific, and I know you won't stop until you find us again. We're doing everything we can to make sure that you do. But there's so much you don't know right now.

I'm trying to be strong. I really am. Please wish us luck.

Love, love, love, Jane

It was impossible not to think about Mom and Dad. There was every reason to believe they'd been on that plane that went over, even if she couldn't know for sure. Watching the giant screen extend over the village and block out the sky had been as hard as anything else up till now.

The strange thing was, Jane understood the other side, too. This was the Nukulas' home. They deserved to protect it. But that didn't make it any easier when she thought about being stuck here for months, or . . . more.

"How long does *Raku Nau* go, anyway?" she whispered to Buzz. "Did anybody say?"

"I don't know," Buzz answered in the dark. It was hard to hear him over the sound of the cicadas and other night creatures that filled the woods around them.

"What if some of us make it and some of us don't?" she asked. "What happens then?"

"You know I don't know any better than you do, so stop asking," Buzz snapped. It wasn't like him to speak harshly to her, but it was better than being treated like a baby. Apparently, those days were gone now. She'd have to keep up with her older siblings and do her best.

And she would.

CHAPTER 8

As the first gray light of morning came on, the *Raku Nau* procession stopped at a clearing in the woods. Carter saw that the trees here were marked all around with more of the red, white, and black paint. Some were striped; others had human and animal figures painted on the bark; and several bore random streaks of color all the way up into the branches. This was a place with some history, he thought.

"Rest here while you can," Ani told them. "It won't be long."

For the moment, all the participants broke off into separate groups. They sat or lay down on the ground, maybe conserving their energy for whatever came next. It had already been a long, difficult walk through the dark.

As usual, the one person who seemed to be alone was the nameless girl from the beach. She sat with her back against a rock, staring into the woods as though she were looking for something.

"Who is that?" Carter asked Ani.

"Her name is Mima," he said.

"Why is she the only one by herself?"

"There are no rules here," Ani answered. "Friendships and cooperation are part of adult leadership, just as they are part of *Raku Nau*."

"So, are you saying she doesn't have any friends?" Carter asked.

"Find out if you want to know," Ani said.

Carter squinted up at him. "How am I supposed to do that?" he asked. "I don't even know how to say hi."

"*Chafa-ka* for a friend, *chafa-ko* for an enemy," Ani said.

"But how do I—" Carter started to say, but Ani cut him off and addressed all four of them now.

"Listen to me. You will be responsible for gathering your own supplies," he said. "All who come into the woods for *Raku Nau* begin with nothing."

"At least it's a level playing field," Vanessa said.

"We're used to working with nothing," Jane added, giving a tired smile.

Carter noticed that the other participants were no longer wearing any jewelry or beads in their hair, as they had been the day before. Their painted faces, however, made it clear who was working with whom. There were groups of three, four, and five, scattered around the camp. Plus Mima.

Without thinking, he reached down in the dirt and swiped a smudge under each of his eyes. He looked at Vanessa, Buzz, and Jane, indicating they should do the same thing

"Now you guys," he said.

Vanessa only shook her head. "Go team," she said sarcastically.

For a second, it felt like a moment from their old life—back when they were a new family of six and always arguing about stupid stuff. But that life didn't even exist anymore, Carter thought. It was a strange emptiness, like a hole in his chest he'd forgotten how to fill.

In the silence, Jane was next to speak up. "Ani?" she asked quietly. You never told us where you're from. Or why you speak English."

It seemed to come out of nowhere, but you never knew what Jane's hundred-mile-an-hour mind was considering at any given time.

"Now, I am from here," Ani answered. "But when I came to this island, I was from Tahiti, where my family spoke both French and English."

"What happened?" Jane asked.

Carter expected Ani to keep his story to himself. But this time, he gave a long answer. It had been a ship fire, out at sea, he explained. Very few had made it off the boat alive, and only he had made it to the island.

He'd been eleven years old—Buzz and Carter's age—when he arrived, after drifting on nothing more than a plank for days. The same currents and tides that had brought Buzz, Jane, Carter, and Vanessa here had brought Ani as well.

"I was nearly dead when the Nukula plucked me from the sea. Soon after that, I became one of them," he said. "I have never wanted for anything here."

"Did you go through *Raku Nau?*" Buzz asked.

Ani paused. "Yes," he said then.

"So where's your *seccu?*" Vanessa asked him.

"His what?" Carter asked.

"I'll tell you later," Vanessa answered.

There seemed to be something she wasn't saying. Something Vanessa knew that the rest of them didn't. But before Carter could ask again, one of the elders came into the middle of the clearing and drew everyone's attention in her direction.

As she began to speak, all of the other participants came onto one knee, with one hand flat on the ground. It looked like some kind of starting position, and Ani gestured for them to do the same.

The woman turned while she addressed the group, motioning with her hands in all four directions, like points on a compass.

"What's she saying?" Carter whispered.

"I don't know," Vanessa said. All the others were

listening, but also fidgeting where they knelt, nudging one another, and, as far as Carter could tell, getting ready to run.

Finally, the male elder stepped forward. He made one sweeping gesture with his hand, as if showing his palm to each of them in turn.

"I think this is it," Carter said.

And then it was. The man let out a long sustained call and dropped his hand to his side. As he did, all the others sprang up and headed straight for the woods. They ran in the same direction the group had been moving all night, farther away from the village.

Carter looked to Ani for any last words.

"Go!" he told them. "Collect what you can. You will need food and water, but more than that, do not be left behind. Remember, you are moving toward Cloud Ridge. The others will call it *Mayamaka*."

"Where is that?" Buzz asked.

"You will see it before long. Try to stay with the group in the meantime," Ani said.

"How are we supposed to do that?" Carter asked. It was all happening too fast. Already, the others were disappearing into the jungle. Some were vaulting up trees, while others ran on the ground.

"Go!" was all Ani gave for an answer. "If you lose the group, it will be over for you before it begins."

It was starting to seem impossible. Maybe it even *was* impossible, but they couldn't help that right now. All Carter could do—all *any* of them could do—was run.

"Let's do this," he said, and they all took off sprinting for the woods.

Jane pushed hard to keep up with the group. As the smallest participant, she also had the shortest legs. The last thing she wanted was to be the reason they fell behind this early in the competition.

Up ahead, most of the other runners had spread out and begun gathering supplies. The first ones they passed were digging some kind of roots out of the ground, brushing off the dirt, and biting right into them. Others were gathered around a small stream, taking drinks.

Jane tried to watch everyone at once, even as she scanned the woods for something they could take as their own.

"Are those bananas?" Buzz asked suddenly. When Jane looked where he was pointing, she saw a heavy bunch of green bananas suspended in a curved leafy tree, straight ahead.

"Carter and Jane, go!" Vanessa said. Already she'd knelt in the dirt next to some plants like the ones the others had been digging up. "Buzz, help me with this."

There was no time to talk. One look from Carter, and Jane raced with him straight over to the banana tree.

The amount of natural food and fresh water here was a million times beyond anything they'd found on Nowhere Island. It wasn't a feast, but a bunch of bananas could make the difference between having enough energy for the journey, or not.

"Get on my back!" Carter said. He bent over with his arms on the trunk. Jane scrambled up until she was standing with her hands higher on the tree, just within reach of the bananas. The trick was going to be getting them down.

"Should I take them all?" Jane said.

"Yes!" he said.

"I'm not sure if I can—"

"Just do it!" he answered. Several of the others had spotted them now and were heading over. They had to get this done quickly.

Jane wrapped her arms around the entire bunch and pulled hard, but the thick stalk didn't budge. At the same time, two other kids appeared at the base of the tree. With a fast leap, they'd each scaled the trunk, holding on with both feet and one hand as they reached for the same bananas.

One of them was Mima, Jane saw, as the girl made a fast grab for the food. Mima easily tore away several bananas and dropped to the ground. The other boy ripped half of what was left from Jane's arms before he, too, jumped off. He landed several feet away and continued on without missing a stride.

There were no rules here—Ani had already told them that. Now that *Raku Nau* had officially begun, Jane could see for herself that this was going to be even harder than she'd thought.

The good news was that the tussle over the bananas had left the remaining seven dangling from the tree. Jane ripped the broken stalk and dropped down next to Carter with what she had.

"I'm sorry," she said. "That's all I could get."

"Don't worry, you did good," Carter said.

Just then, a nearby shout caught Jane's attention. It was Mima again. The girl stood empty-handed now. She was yelling after Chizo and one of his friends as they ran off, laughing and clutching the bananas that she'd been holding just a moment ago.

"Come on," Jane told Carter, and approached the girl where she stood catching her breath.

"Here," Jane said. She tore off two pieces of fruit from their own seven and held them out. Carter didn't say a word. Jane knew he wouldn't mind.

Mima looked up at them with a suspicious glance. She made no move to take the bananas.

"Chafa-ka," Jane said. She pointed to herself then, and spoke her own name slowly. "Jane," she said, and pointed to her brother. "Carter."

The girl looked at her again. Then she snatched the

bananas out of her hand with a nod, and ran off.

"You're welcome," Jane said quietly.

"We have to go!" Carter said. "Buzz! Vanessa! Come on!"

The rest of the group was moving again, headed down a V-shaped cut in the hillside where two slopes came together. Jane could hear rushing water in the distance, but couldn't see what was waiting for them that way.

"What'd you get?" Vanessa asked, running with Buzz to join them. The two each had a small handful of tubular roots, still half covered in dirt. The bananas were rock hard. It wasn't going to be much of a breakfast, and they'd have to eat on the run. But they'd had worse on Nowhere Island. As long as they didn't have to go back to eating grubs and snails, Jane thought, she wasn't going to complain.

She could just see Mima now, not on the ground but leaping from trunk to trunk using her arms and legs like bumpers. Just before she disappeared down the hill, she took a long jump to the ground, then kept on running.

"What's our strategy?" Buzz asked. Most of the group had disappeared in the same direction. This was a fast-moving game.

Except—not a game at all, Jane thought.

"Our strategy is *keep up!*" Carter said, and led the way downhill. "Let's *go!*"

CHAPTER 9

Buzz ran with the others, following the stream they'd drunk from. It flowed down the ravine and toward the louder water sounds.

"What is that?" Carter asked.

The stream ran straight into a river at the bottom of the hill, where the woods ended. As they reached the bank, they were facing a high wall of sand-colored stone on the opposite side. The river itself ran along the wall as far as Buzz could see in either direction. But the water also flowed into a narrow canyon, almost directly across from them.

That's where the others seemed to be headed. They

entered the canyon single file, squeezing one by one through the opening before each of them disappeared inside.

"How do they know that's the right way to go?" Buzz asked. It wasn't even a canyon, really. More like a crevice. There was no knowing what waited inside. The only other way to go was downriver or upriver, and that looked to be a mile or more in either direction, just to get around the mountain of rock that stood in front of them.

"Maybe they're guessing," Jane said, "But their guess is better than ours."

"Keep going!" Carter said. "And watch your step!"

The river was shallow but shady, with green algae-covered stones everywhere. Buzz felt his foot slip on the first one he came to.

Vanessa grabbed him under the arm. "Don't go too fast," she said. "You could break an ankle in here pretty easily."

Buzz focused on his steps and tried not to think too much about what came next. Even from here, the slot canyon looked claustrophobic.

When they reached the far side, Carter and Jane didn't slow down. They pushed right in.

Vanessa looked at Buzz and took a deep breath. He could tell she was uneasy, too, but neither of them said a word. Most of the other runners were already inside, and the last group was just starting to cross the river. This was no time to hesitate. Vanessa went next, behind Jane and Carter. Buzz brought up the rear.

It was like stepping through a door and into a narrow hallway. The crevice walls on either side were nearly vertical, and they were close enough to touch with both hands.

"Can you see anything?" Vanessa called out to Carter.

"Not much," he called back.

Buzz craned his neck, but it was too shadowy in the canyon, and too crowded with runners to see more than backs of people's heads. Their shouts and even some laughter echoed back and forth, filling the small space with sound.

The closeness of the rock was uncomfortable, but

it also made it easier to stay upright. When Buzz stumbled, one quick catch with his palm was enough to keep himself moving along, faster than he'd imagined might be possible in here.

Which was a good thing. The four runners behind him were in close now. He could tell they were looking for the first opportunity to pass.

Soon, they all came to a fork. Where the canyon divided, the water flowed in two different directions. For whatever reason, everyone in front of them had gone to the right. Carter, Jane, and Vanessa did the same, followed by Buzz and the four others breathing down his neck.

They hadn't gotten much father when a voice from up ahead echoed back, louder than all the others.

"FAH!"

It was Chizo, Buzz recognized. He and his friends must have been at the front. *Fah* meant no, which probably meant they'd reached a dead end.

The whole line came to a quick stop. Buzz had to put on the brakes to keep from running right into Vanessa.

"What's going on?" she asked.

"I don't know," Carter answered. "Jane, get on my shoulders. See if you can tell anything from here."

Jane jumped up on a rock, then stepped right onto Carter's back. She was already the best climber in the family, and getting better at it all the time.

"It looks like they're turning around," she said. Even as she spoke, Buzz could see several runners coming back the other way. Definitely a dead end.

"GO, go, go!" Carter said, letting Jane down and waving at the others to backtrack.

Buzz turned one-eighty and kept moving. Two seconds ago, they'd been the second-to-last team in the canyon. Now, with the whole line reversed, they were second from the front. Maybe it was a temporary advantage, but they'd take every little boost they could get.

It wasn't long before they were back at the same fork. To the left was the way out, and to the right, another unknown tributary.

"Which way?" Buzz asked. "Back outside, or over here?" He pointed to the right, where the four Nukula who were now ahead of them had just gone.

The question was, what would everyone else do? If they all started going different ways, it seemed best to stick with the majority.

"Let's let a few more people go first, and see what they do," Vanessa said.

"No way!" Carter called back. "Don't slow down while we're ahead!"

As they stood there, three more Nukula scrambled past. They used the rocks and the side walls to vault themselves forward through the vertical space before Buzz or any of his siblings could stop them. Then they cut left and headed back out of the canyon.

"Are you satisfied?" Carter said. "We're already losing our lead. Now *go!*"

Buzz turned and took the right fork. This was no time to fuss over decisions. It was a go-for-broke situation, not a video game you could put on pause. If the Nukula weren't stopping to consider every move, then Buzz couldn't afford to, either.

Which only amped up the pressure.

The crevice twisted immediately left, and then back

again. Each turn was narrower than the one before. It was getting tighter by the second. And then he heard a familiar call up ahead.

"FAH!" yelled whoever was at the front now. This time, Buzz could easily see where the rock walls came together. They were running toward another dead end.

"We have to go back!" he said. He turned to go, but it was clear that the people pressing in behind Vanessa, Jane, and Carter didn't want to turn around a second time. They tried to squeeze by, but there was no room here.

Chizo and his two friends were shouting from behind now, waving for them to keep going.

"We can't!" Carter shouted back, and pointed for them to reverse direction, but it was no good. They pushed in, harder. Several people stumbled forward, squeezing the line into an even smaller space than before.

The group piled in from both sides now. Buzz's chest tightened, and his stomach dropped. It was getting harder to breathe, and there was nothing he could do as arms, bodies, and immovable rock walls pressed in around him.

Carter kept one hand on the rock to steady himself. The other hand was clamped onto Jane's shoulder.

"Carter?" she said.

"I've got you!" he said. He crouched over Jane just to keep her from being crushed. Every second, there was less room to move in the tiny space. Someone tried to push by, and he pushed back—only to get another, harder shove from some unseen hand or elbow.

"I can't breathe!" Jane called out.

"Just hang on!" he said.

Carter's heart clenched. There was nothing more he could do to protect her. The ones at the front were trying to double back, and the ones at the back hadn't gotten through their thick heads that there was no way to keep going in this direction. The jam couldn't last forever, but so far nobody was giving any ground.

"MOVE!" he yelled at the girl right behind him. But there was nowhere for her to go. He could hear Chizo yelling something from the other end as well. It was too crowded even to see anymore.

Then something caught him at the back of the head with three quick jabs. It was the last straw. Carter looked around fast, ready to take a real swing at someone.

"Car-tare!" a voice called from just above. He looked up, and Mima was there. She hung suspended at least five feet off the ground, her feet and hands pressed against either side of the crevice.

"Car-tare! Jane!" she said, and jerked her chin to show which way she was headed—straight up. When Carter looked, he could see a line of blue sky, maybe thirty feet over their heads.

As usual, there was no knowing about right and wrong decisions. There was only his gut, and now his gut was saying that they should follow Mima. He'd been right about her so far, anyway.

"Buzz! Vanessa!" he yelled. Mima had already begun working her way higher. "Jane, come on! You first."

Jane scrambled onto his shoulders again. She pressed her hands against the rock, then stepped off with one foot and the other, wedging herself between the walls as Mima had done. A second later, she slid both feet up the rock a short distance, pushed herself higher with her arms, and continued that way, starting her own climb toward the top.

"Buzz, can you do this?" Carter asked. His brother didn't look too confident.

"Do we have any choice?" Buzz asked.

"Go ahead, then. I'll be right behind you."

"You mean under me," Buzz said grimly, as he started to climb.

Most of the others had jumped onto the same idea by now. When Carter looked again, he saw two dozen bodies silhouetted against the light, like a mass of giant spiders working their way up the walls.

"There's some handholds, too!" Carter called. "Use whatever you can!" He reached up and guided Buzz's foot toward a small ledge.

"I've got it, I've got it!" Buzz said. Even here, he didn't seem to want Carter telling him what to do. But they had to get out of this canyon, whatever it took. Carter made sure to follow Buzz's path from below, just in case he needed a save.

His own hand throbbed as he worked. The cut had begun to heal, but the pressure of the climb was not helping. As he pushed himself another foot higher on the rock, his palm left behind a red smear of blood.

"You guys okay?" Jane called down.

"Fine. Keep going!" Carter yelled to her. "Just try to get to the—

"*Ekka-ko!*" a shout came from above, and then the familiar sound of Chizo's obnoxious laugh. Carter looked just in time to see him kicking something off a ledge near the top. It barely registered, until the shower of rock and gravel started down.

"Jane, look out!" he said.

Carter's eyes filled with dust. Several small stones bounced painfully off his back and shoulders. And then, even worse, he heard Jane's scream.

"I can't hold on!" she said.

"Vanessa, help her!" Carter shouted back. His vision was blurred, and his grip was shaky. He could still hear Chizo and the others laughing, too.

"I'm coming!" Vanessa called out, but then almost right away—"Jane! NO!"

Carter swiped at his eyes with the back of his arm. Before he could see anything, he heard a gasp, and felt another shower of gravel.

"Thank you!" Jane's voice came then, just as his vision started to clear. He could see Mima and Jane now, ten or twelve feet over his head. Mima's feet were pressed against the side walls, with both hands free. She had Jane's arm hooked into her own, and held her there, swinging in midair. For a crazy moment, it reminded Carter of the barrel of monkeys he had played with when he was a little kid.

"Are you okay?" Carter choked out. His eyes stung, and everyone was coughing from the dust.

"I've got it," Jane said as she found her footing. "Let's keep going." Her voice was set with determination. She wasn't going to let herself be the baby anymore—that much was clear. But she was still his little sister.

As he started up again, Carter couldn't stop thinking about Chizo. Ani had warned them that the others would try to slow them down—whatever it took. Well, that was a two-way street, wasn't it?

If there was any doubt before, it was gone now. Chizo

was enemy number one. And he was going to pay for what he'd done.

As Jane reached the top of the canyon walls, it was a relief just to feel the sun on her face again. It told her she'd made it.

She gripped the top edge of the crevice on one side, swung her leg up, and rolled onto flat ground—all without anyone's help. Mima stood there, just watching, as though she already knew Jane could finish it on her own.

"Thank you for saving me down there!" Jane gasped out, still catching her breath. "I wish I knew how to say that in Nukula."

It seemed maybe the gift of bananas had meant something. While the other runners started off again, Mima stayed put. She wasn't leaving without them. Not so far, anyway.

As Jane looked around, she saw that the plateau where they now stood was crisscrossed with cracks in the ground. Each one was another crevice, like a maze that cut through this mountain of rock. It was clear now that they never would have found their way through. Up and out was the only solution.

As Vanessa, Buzz, and Carter reached the top, Jane knelt down to help them.

"Where is he?" Carter asked, the moment he was up.

"Who?" Vanessa asked

"Chizo! He tried to knock us off that wall on purpose! You know he did!"

"Chizo," Mima repeated, and pointed to the other runners in the distance. Jane could see Chizo and his friends at the front of the pack. *"Ekka-ko,"* Mima added.

Ani had said that *ka* was for friends, and *ko* was for enemies. It seemed as though Mima didn't like Chizo any more than Carter did.

"This is Vanessa, and this is Buzz," Jane said slowly, pointing to each of them for Mima's benefit.

"Buzz, Ba-nessa, Car-tare, Jane," Mima said quickly, and then tilted her head toward the horizon. There was no time for talking. They had to keep moving.

When Jane took one last look into the crevice, it

was empty. She thought about the runners who had taken the other fork down below. Would she see them again? Or had their own odds of succeeding at *Raku Nau* just gotten a little bit better?

"This way?" Carter asked, pointing after the runners.

"Mayamaka," Mima said. She pointed into the distance as they set out. There, across an open valley that stretched for miles ahead, stood a high, jagged ridge. Its top edge was barely visible through a shroud of fog and mist.

"I guess that's where we're going," Vanessa said. "Cloud Ridge."

"Yeah," Carter said. "Maya . . ."

"Mayamaka," the girl repeated without slowing down.

Jane jogged behind, trying not to think about how far they still had to go. Looking across the valley to where the ridge loomed in the distance, it was hard to imagine finishing *Raku Nau* at all. Much less ahead of half the group.

"How are we going to do this?" she blurted out. "I just don't see how—"

"We don't have a choice, Jane," Vanessa cut her off. "All we can do is keep moving and try to stay positive."

"We didn't give up before," Carter said. "And we aren't going to now."

"I know," Jane said, but the lump in her throat made it hard to talk. There was no way to feel good about this. Their only choices were stopping and continuing on.

And when she thought about it that way, she realized there was no real choice at all.

CHAPTER 16

Vanessa knew Jane was right. The odds of getting to Cloud Ridge in time to win four of the sixteen *seccu* were somewhere around zero. But she couldn't admit that to Carter, Buzz, and Jane.

She thought about Nowhere Island again. Nothing had been harder than that. A hundred times out there, she'd thought there was no way they were going to make it. But looking back, she realized, she'd gotten through by taking it one thing at a time. Slowing her breath down when it spiked. Focusing on the task at hand. Using her time and energy as efficiently as she could.

And right now, the best thing she could do was stop worrying and concentrate on memorizing as much of the landscape as possible.

Behind them, she could see the jungle they'd just come through. Straight ahead, across the valley, was the mountain Ani had told them about, Cloud Ridge. Its top looked like a giant crown, with several thin peaks that rose up into the mist.

It was clear they wouldn't be staying on this high ground for long. They were going to have to climb back down at some point. Then across the valley and back up again, to the top of Cloud Ridge before they'd even have a chance of getting to the far shore, and away.

The few bananas and roots they'd eaten weren't going to be enough, either. There was food to worry about, and water, along with sleep, and whatever dangers this landscape was still hiding from them.

One thing at a time, Diaz, she thought. That was all she could ever do. That, and make absolutely sure nobody got lost or left behind.

"Does this go on all day and night?" Buzz asked as they jogged along.

"I wish I knew," Vanessa said. "We have to sleep sometime."

"Yeah, just not right now," Carter said. Since the canyon, he'd been watching the runners ahead with that familiar squint of his. Vanessa could tell what he was thinking with one glance.

"Carter, we have to stay focused. Don't do anything stupid about Chizo, okay?" she said.

"Why not?" he said. "He deserves something stupid to happen to him."

"Why not? Because you're not the only one in this family!" she said. "How many times do you need me to say it?"

"And how many times do I have to tell you, you're not in charge!" Carter shot back.

Mima looked over at them, shook her head, and kept on running. If she ever decided to pull away, they were going to have to pick up their pace. But right now, it was all they could do to go at a jog. The climb had left all four of them flagging.

Vanessa took a deep breath. "I'm serious," she said. "Getting back at Chizo isn't going to help us get any farther. And it's not going to impress Mima, either, by the way."

Carter glared at her. "Who said anything about impressing Mima?" he asked.

It was obvious he had a crush on this girl. He'd run after her from the moment she showed up on the beach.

"She's probably, like, two years older than you," Vanessa told him.

"I bet she's not," Carter said.

"So you *are* trying to impress her?" Vanessa asked.

"Shut up, Vanessa," Carter said, and surged ahead as they all moved toward the edge of the plateau.

"I'll take that as a yes!" Vanessa called out. But Carter didn't even look back.

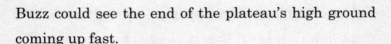

Buzz could see the end of the plateau's high ground coming up fast.

All of the other runners had already stopped along the edge. They were clustered in one spot, between two gnarled evergreens that seemed to grow right out of the rock. Everyone was looking down at something as Buzz, Vanessa, Carter, Jane, and Mima caught up to the group.

"What is it?" Buzz asked, tapping Mima on the shoulder. He knew they didn't speak the same language, but sometimes it was easier just to say what he was thinking, whether or not Mima understood.

When she pointed, her answer was clear enough. Halfway down the cliff, water gushed out from one of the crevices and splashed into a perfectly round, deep green pool below. The pounding sound of the falls was a low roar from where Buzz stood. They'd been traveling uphill since getting out of the canyon, and the drop from here looked to be about fifty feet.

"We're going to have to look for somewhere to climb down," Jane said.

"Actually . . ." Buzz said. He could sense something from the way everyone was eyeing the drop-off. "I don't think it's going to be a climb."

"You mean, jump?" Carter asked. "How do we even know it's deep enough down there?"

Vanessa pointed at their feet. On the ground, three

red lines, three white lines, and three black lines were painted onto the rock. It was like Nukula graffiti.

"Buzz is right," she said. "I think this is the way to go. I just wish it wasn't."

Buzz took a deep breath. The idea of jumping sent a shiver right through him.

Chizo called over then and said something that made several of the others laugh. When Buzz looked up, they were all staring right at him.

His face went hot. Was it obvious that he was the weak link? Was his fear showing right on his face? He tried to ignore Chizo and his friends, but it was impossible. This wasn't the first time he'd been made fun of. Usually it happened in gym, or at recess. Now, it was as if he'd traveled six thousand miles from home, just to get the same kind of treatment.

Whatever it was Chizo had said, Mima shouted something right back. Carter lunged their way, but Vanessa grabbed him by the arm.

"Carter—don't!" she said. "I'm serious."

Before anyone could make another move, Mima called out again. Everyone stopped what they were doing and looked at her. She backed up then, took a deep breath, and, without any further warning, reversed direction. In three fast running strides, she took a leap that sent her hurtling out over the edge.

Buzz felt his heart jump right along with her.

"Mima!" Jane called. All four of them looked over the side of the plateau. She fell with arms spinning and toes pointed until she hit the white water at the base of the falls and disappeared.

"Do you see her?" Vanessa asked.

"No," Carter said.

"Not yet," Jane said.

Several others were murmuring in Nukula, too. It seemed as though everyone was waiting to see how Mima had fared before they tried the jump themselves.

Buzz counted silently. *One, two, three, four—*

"How deep do you think that pool is?" Jane said.

—five, six, seven—

"Maybe she hit a rock," Vanessa said.

—eight, nine, ten, eleven, twelve—

With every count, it seemed more and more as though something terrible had happened. But then—

"There!" Jane said. She pointed to the edge of the green pool, where Mima had just surfaced. Mima swam a few strokes, then stood up in the shallower water and walked up onto the shore.

Buzz let out the breath he'd been holding, and Jane squeezed his hand. He felt a little proud, too. Mima was a part of their team now. It felt like a victory. And more than that, it was a reason to push himself even harder.

He thought about their dad, Eric Diaz. Buzz remembered him talking about going bungee jumping in college. *You can't wait until you're not scared,* Dad had said. *And you can't think twice. You just have to go.* The ones who waited were the ones who let the fear get the best of them and sometimes chickened out. The trick, Dad always said, was jumping in spite of being afraid.

Dad's words echoed through his mind. *Don't think twice.* Buzz was already afraid to jump. And now, literally, he was on his way to his second thought about it—the one he might never come back from. Before it could even take shape in his mind, he called out to the others.

"I'll go next," he said.

It was the only way.

"Are you sure?" Vanessa said. "Do you want one of us to—"

"I don't want to talk about it," he said. His chin shook with the next breath, but he was determined. He swallowed once, bent his knees, and got ready to leap.

At the same moment, there was a stirring behind them. Someone let out a low growling sound, and Buzz heard footsteps coming closer. He turned and saw that Chizo was making a go at it, too.

Buzz instinctively stepped back. Chizo shot past him, too close. Buzz's impulse to move out of the way quickly turned into a stumble. One foot slipped over the rock, and out into thin air.

"Buzz!"

Vanessa reached for him. Carter lunged. But it was too late. Gravity took hold as he slid several inches toward the edge—and then off it.

The next thing Buzz knew, he was falling.

Carter couldn't believe what he'd just seen. One second, Buzz was there, and the next, he'd dropped out of sight right behind Chizo.

All they could do was stare horrified over the edge. Buzz flailed with his arms as he fell. It looked as if he was trying to get upright in the air, but there wasn't enough time. His back slapped the water with a smack that sounded all the way up to the top, and made Carter cringe.

"Buzz!" Vanessa shouted.

"Buzz!" Jane said. "Is he okay?"

Carter tensed all over. Buzz had disappeared at the base of the falls. It took several long seconds before he surfaced, and even then, he seemed disoriented.

Mima had waded back into the pool. She motioned for him to swim toward her, and he took a few ragged strokes, but then stopped again. When he looked up, a grimace of pain showed on his face.

Chizo, meanwhile, was still in the pool. He watched from a distance, backstroking slowly toward the opposite side, like he was enjoying the show.

Chizo! Just the thought of his name made Carter

burn. The anger rose up inside him and boiled over.

"I'm going to kill him!" he yelled.

He sprang up and away from the edge. His vision tunneled. All he saw was the open air ahead of him. He drove with his feet—one, two, three, four lunging steps—

"Carter, no!" Vanessa yelled, half a second too late.

The fall was the worst part. Carter felt like he was leaving his stomach behind as he plummeted toward the green pool.

He dropped, faster and faster, spinning his arms until he hit the surface. It was like breaking through glass, followed by the shock of freezing water. Even then, he didn't stop. His body plunged deeper than he ever would have imagined.

Disoriented, Carter knew from experience that he had to look for the light. He turned around in the water until he'd spotted the surface, and then kicked toward it.

By the time he emerged, his lungs felt ready to explode. The falls poured down like liquid concrete on his head, and he fought to swim out of the way as the backflow tried to keep him where he was.

While he swam, other jumpers started hitting the

water around him. They splashed down on his left and right like human torpedoes. He saw Jane land, then Vanessa. And then, closer by, there was Chizo. He was still in the pool, and still watching them.

Carter didn't think. He lunged through the water. Chizo did, too, and they met in the middle, grappling against each other.

There was no time to worry about the others. Carter's only focus was Chizo. He grabbed on with both arms, the way Chizo had done to him the day before. But Chizo was slippery in the water. He twisted around, pulled one arm free and then the other.

Before Carter could make another move, the whole thing flipped. Chizo had him now, and he squeezed hard. He held Carter from behind in a painful bear hug as they dropped beneath the surface once more.

Carter roared underwater. He squirmed and pulled. But it was no good. Chizo knew how to keep this hold locked down in a way that Carter hadn't. It was like some kind of unbreakable wrestling move. And whatever air Carter had left in his lungs, it was a good bet that Chizo had more.

Then someone else was there. And another. Carter felt a tussle going on around him. He couldn't tell what was happening until he recognized Buzz and Vanessa through the blur of the water. They each had two hands on one of Chizo's arms, pulling him away like human crowbars.

Slowly, Chizo's grip loosened. Carter broke free, and all of them surfaced at the same time.

He'd barely gotten his next breath before he was reaching for Chizo. His only thought was to do as much damage as he could. Chizo grinned back, his half-red, half-black painted face now a monster mask of running colors.

"Don't do it!" Vanessa yelled in Carter's ear. Carter strained, but she and Buzz pulled him away with a force that surprised him.

"He's too strong!" Buzz screamed. "You can't take him! Let's go!"

Chizo was treading water and watching them. But Carter also noticed he wasn't coming closer. Maybe he could beat one of them at a time, but not all three. Not the whole family.

"This isn't over!" Carter shouted at him.

"Come on!" Vanessa said. "We're ahead of them! Let's just go!"

Not all of Chizo's group was down yet, Carter realized. Vanessa was right. This was a chance to move ahead. Reluctantly, he turned and swam toward Mima and Jane at the edge of the pool.

"Are you hurt, Buzz?" he asked, as they stumbled out of the water. Carter could see the stop-sign-red streaks up and down Buzz's back. It looked like the world's worst sunburn, but Buzz only shrugged.

"It doesn't matter," he answered. More than anything, he looked focused. Which was what Carter needed to be now, too.

"This way?" Vanessa asked Mima. She pointed into the woods, but Mima pointed downriver instead. From here, the water flowed out of the green pool, along the edge of the forest, and out of sight.

"*Dis way,*" Mima said. "*Ekka-ka!*"

Ekka-ka, Carter thought. *Ka,* for a friend.

At least there was that.

CHAPTER 11

As they moved along the river, Carter stuck with Jane, Vanessa, Buzz, and Mima. It wasn't long before Chizo and his friends passed them, but they never lost sight of the larger group. By his count, there were twenty-eight runners still in it. Somewhere along the way, four had been left behind.

Before long, the river led them to the mouth of a bay that cut into the island's coastline. The bay was several hundred yards across, with more jungle rimming the far shore. Beyond that, Carter could just see the spiked peaks of Cloud Ridge in the distance.

"What's that?" Buzz asked. He pointed farther up

the beach, where a tall wooden post was planted in the sand. It wasn't hard to recognize the red, black, and white markings of *Raku Nau* by now. They were faded but noticeable, as though the post had been painted a long time ago. Its wood was worn smooth in places, and the top was hatched in a kind of zigzag pattern.

Most of the Nukula seemed to know something about it. They glanced in its direction several times as they began spreading out along the shore.

"Are we making camp?" Jane asked hopefully.

"It looks that way," Vanessa said. She pointed over to where Mima had already begun picking up dry wood. The other groups seemed to be staking out different sites for the night.

Carter didn't say much, but it was a relief to stop. The sun was headed for the horizon, and it would be dark before too long.

He kept his eye on Chizo as they worked, and he thought about everything he wished he could do to wipe the conceited look off that kid's face. Back home, Chizo probably would have been in high school, or at least eighth grade. Carter was big and strong for his age, but he was still a few months shy of middle school.

At least, he *would* start middle school if he ever got home again. Back to the other side of the world.

"Car-tare!" Mima called over. She had been working her way up the shore, but now she set down her pile of firewood and was motioning for him to come over.

"What is it?" he asked, as he reached her.

She held out her hand to show him a ball of greenish mud. Without pausing, she took him by the wrist and pressed the mud into the cut on his hand.

"Ow! What are you doing?" he asked.

It stung as she rubbed it in, working it down to a kind of second skin that covered the wound. When she was done, she put the rest of the mud ball—it was really more like clay—into his other hand, and pointed across the bay.

"What?" he asked.

"You're supposed to take it with you," Jane said.

Carter hadn't even known Jane had followed him over. She was pretty good at sneaking around when she wanted to.

He looked down at the mud again, and then across the bay.

"That way?" he asked. "That's where we go tomorrow? Straight across?"

"That's a long swim," Jane said.

Carter nodded and put the mud into his side pocket. But now Mima was laughing for some reason.

"What?" he asked again, shrugging to show his meaning.

Mima plucked a waxy leaf off a low bush from the edge of the woods. It was the size of her palm, and she held it out.

"*Ekka, Car-tare*," she said. He liked her knowing his name, anyway. But mostly he felt stupid for not knowing he should have wrapped the mud in a leaf.

"Thanks," he said, looking down while his face burned a little.

Way to go, Benson, he thought. *All smooth, all the time.*

When he looked up again, Mima had already turned away. She was looking at something out toward the ocean.

Several others had taken notice, too, and were

heading over. That's when Carter saw Ani, and the two elders from before. They were rowing an outrigger in from the open water. Behind them was a simple bamboo raft, tethered to their boat.

"What's going on?" Jane said. Buzz and Vanessa were there now, along with all the other runners. The energy in the camp had just jumped. Something was about to happen, and as far as Carter could tell, Jane, Vanessa, Buzz, and he were the only ones who didn't know what it was.

Vanessa watched as Ani and the others paddled closer. Then, just as she expected them to come to shore, they turned and aimed themselves for the middle of the wide bay.

"Ani! What's happening?" she called out, not even expecting him to reply.

What he did was turn to face the group on the shore while the other two paddled. He reached down and picked something up from the floor of the outrigger. It was a painted and carved piece of wood, some kind of animal figure. Its markings were immediately familiar. The striped pattern matched the ones on the post that sat farther up the beach. And in fact, Vanessa realized, they were like puzzle pieces. The sawtooth cut at the base of the totem in Ani's hand was the same as the zigzag pattern cut into the top of the post.

"They go together," Jane said, recognizing it, too.

Ani began speaking then, but in Nukula. All the runners on either side of Vanessa knelt at the water's edge, with one palm flat on the ground. It was like the start of *Raku Nau,* all over again. She took up the same position with her siblings.

Vanessa couldn't help feeling more nervous than ever. She looked to Mima, who seemed calm, or at least focused. That helped a little. They'd have to follow along and figure this out—whatever it was— once it started.

But then Ani gave them the few words in English they needed to understand.

"The first to place the totem atop the post on the beach will be free to use the raft however he or she wishes," he called out.

All at once, the stakes went up. Vanessa eyed the far side of the bay. Knowing they'd be traveling in that direction, it was clear now just how much they needed the advantage of the raft. Swimming across would be exhausting. Hiking all the way around could take hours of extra time they didn't have.

It was also a chance to do something for Mima. She'd started *Raku Nau* on her own, but this was a challenge that no one person was going to be able to complete alone.

Finally, Ani held the wooden piece high over his head. He pulled the raft closer, placed the totem in the middle of its deck, and then untied the vine-rope tether from the outrigger.

"Ma tikka sematikka!" he shouted. "By any means necessary!"

With that, he dropped the rope and set the raft free. At the same moment, all twenty-eight runners sprinted into the water, including Vanessa, Carter, Jane, Buzz—and, at the front of the pack, Mima.

Even as Buzz splashed into the chill water with the others, he thought about what Ani had just said: *By any means necessary*. This was going to get ugly, he could tell.

"Vanessa, Jane, stay here!" Carter said to the girls as they swam out. "We need a line of defense. Buzz, come with me!"

Buzz didn't question it. He let Carter call the shots and focused instead on what they had to do.

Looking back, he saw that several of the others had done the same. Chizo was headed for the raft, but two of his group were treading water nearby, halfway between the raft and the red, black, and white post on the shore.

It was a long swim. Buzz quickly fell behind, but he didn't stop. By the time he reached the raft, all of the others were swarming around it. Three of them—two boys and a girl—had climbed up on top. All three had their hands on the totem, trying to pull it loose from one another. Everyone else seemed to be waiting to see who came up with it first.

It seemed like a hugely uneven contest. The groups were all different sizes, and Chizo was obviously one of the strongest in the competition, if not *the* strongest. But then again, there were lots of things about the Nukula that were hard to understand. Not necessarily better or worse, just different.

"Over there!" Carter said. Buzz swam again, following him around to the back of the raft where it was less crowded.

"Wait here!" Carter told him. He didn't know what Carter had in mind, but it was a relief just to catch his breath for a second.

Carter had barely pulled himself up onto the raft deck before one of the girls reached out and shoved him off with both hands. He plunged in, popped right back up, and jumped on board again. This time Mima was beside him. They both stayed low, which Buzz saw made it harder to push them off.

"Get it!" he yelled. The adrenaline was pumping. He could feel himself rising to the challenge.

Carter was on his knees now, both hands on the totem. With a fast jerk, he pulled it free from the other three and fell onto his back on the raft. Mima was right there to take it from him.

"YES!" Buzz shouted out.

It didn't last long. Before she could even dive, the whole raft rose up in the water. Chizo and two others were there, underneath, raising it into a hard tilt that sent everyone on top sprawling.

Mima fell right toward Buzz, still holding the totem, but it slipped out of her hands when she splashed into the water next to him.

This was his chance. Buzz wrapped his arms around the rough wooden piece and dove down under the surface. If he could disappear with it, even for a few seconds, it might buy them an edge.

He kicked toward the shore, eyes open underwater as a dozen pair of legs twisted around in every direction. They were looking for him, he could tell. His heart surged—he was actually getting somewhere. But there was no way it could last, and he knew it.

He kicked for several more yards, until his lungs couldn't take another moment. Then he aimed for an open place in the water and surfaced.

The swarm was on him immediately.

"Carter!" he yelled. "Mima!"

Before he could spot them, one of Chizo's teammates enveloped Buzz with both arms and pulled him under. There was no contest now. A second later, the boy had yanked the totem from his grasp and was headed toward shore.

They were getting closer to the beach, Buzz realized. All the participants who had hung back were heading toward the swimmers for another face-off. Carter and Mima were swimming ahead of Buzz. He was exhausted, with arms like rubber, but there was no way he could give up now.

As Chizo's teammate moved toward the center of the action, he was met by a storm of opposition. Mima grabbed him from behind and took him under, followed quickly by several others piling on. The water churned. It looked like a piranha feeding frenzy.

Buzz stopped long enough to take stock, and Mima popped up just in front of him, clutching the totem to her chest.

"HERE!" Carter screamed. "Here!" He'd pulled a football move—even Buzz recognized it. Carter had gone wide, away from the group. Mima pivoted and seemed to spot him. She shouldered the totem and tossed it high over the others' heads—only to have it intercepted at the last second by another girl, the tallest Nukula in the group. As soon as the girl had the totem, she turned and started running for shore.

One of the other boys was the first to get to her. He threw a tackle from behind, and they went down in the shallow water. Jane and Vanessa were in it now, too, with Carter coming in fast.

Within seconds, the entire group was scrambling in the same spot. It gave Buzz enough time to catch up, but by then, it was like trying to break through a wall even to see the totem anymore.

"Buzz! Here!" Vanessa screamed. He saw her then, holding the piece by her fingertips. Somehow she'd reached the edge of the group with it, but not for long. Chizo was there to snatch it. He pulled it out of her hands—just before Mima blindsided him from behind. She leaped onto his back, grabbed the totem, slid off, and kept moving.

"Run!" Carter called to her. She'd bought just a few feet of advantage, and it was enough to get her sprinting the last few yards onto the beach.

But it wasn't over. Everyone was headed out of the water now. Buzz felt himself jostled and pushed along, nearly against his will. Carter was on his right, and Chizo was just ahead. Without any plan, both of them grabbed onto Chizo from behind, each taking an arm.

All three boys hit the sand hard. Buzz felt both of the others roll over him—and then they were on their feet again, faster than he ever could have managed.

Meanwhile, Mima had made some good headway. With the totem tucked under one arm, she'd climbed onto Vanessa's shoulders and leaped from there to a point more than halfway up the fifteen-foot post. Others were scrambling behind her, but she still had a good lead. She shimmied several feet higher. Jane and Vanessa were pulling on the legs of those who were either climbing or reaching to yank Mima down. Carter and Chizo were both sprinting to join the fray.

As Buzz watched, Mima covered that last few feet to the top. She took hold of the post with both legs to free up her hands—and dropped the zigzag edge of the totem into place.

At the same moment, one of the boys managed to get a hold of her ankle. With a hard grab, he pulled her right off, and they both fell in a heap to the sand.

Buzz's eyes were locked on the top of the post. It seemed everyone else's were, too. As Mima had fallen, the whole post had jerked to the side. Now, the totem rocked one way . . . and back again, ready to tip all the way off, or not.

Buzz held his breath. He could feel the pulse pounding in his throat. The whole beach seemed to go silent—just before the totem rocked once more and and fell cleanly into place, where it stayed.

"YES!" Carter screamed. He threw his arms around Jane and spun her around. Vanessa grabbed Mima by the hand and helped her onto her feet as Buzz ran over. Even Mima was smiling now.

Looking at the faces of everyone else around them, Buzz could see they all seemed to be thinking the same thing. Nobody—including himself—could believe they'd just pulled this off.

But guess what? Buzz thought. *We did it.*

And right now, that was all that mattered.

CHAPTER 12

Jane lay back and watched the starry night sky from their precious new raft. With the mat of leaves Mima had shown them how to make, it was a comfortable place to get some rest. Not only had they won a way to paddle across the bay in the morning, but they'd earned a bed in the process.

Not that any of them felt perfectly safe. They'd already agreed to take turns keeping watch through the night. Jane would stay up first, then Vanessa, then Carter, then Buzz. Jane wasn't sure what Mima would do, but so far, she'd been sticking close.

She looked over, where Mima was adding some

wood to the fire. Mima had been the one to build it, too, using some bamboo, a sharp stick, and dry grass. On Nowhere Island, they'd never once managed to get a flame like that, no matter how hard they'd tried. Mima had done it in about ten minutes.

In a way, Mima seemed amazing. But in another way, Jane thought, she was just Nukula. This was normal for them. This was her life.

Still, Jane was full of questions.

"Mima?" she said. She picked up one of the smaller sticks from the firewood pile. It wasn't a pen, but it was as close as she was going to get.

With the stick, she drew six simple figures—four small and two big. Then she pointed at them one by one. "Jane, Buzz, Carter, Vanessa," she said. And then, pointing at the two big ones, "Mom and Dad."

Jane held out the stick for her, but Mima only squinted.

"Now you," Jane said.

"*Fah,*" Mima said and turned back to the fire.

"*Ah-ka-ah!*" Jane said. "Please?" It was a thrill, to actually be having a conversation, even if Mima didn't seem so interested. Still, Jane held out the stick again, and this time Mima took it.

In the sand next to Jane's family, Mima drew an even simpler figure. It was just a circle and a line for a body. When she was done, she dropped the stick in the fire.

"You?" Jane asked, pointing at the drawing. "Mima?"

"Mima," she answered.

"You don't have any family?" Jane asked.

"She can't understand you," Carter said from where he lay on the raft.

"Yes she can," Jane said. She looked down at the single stick figure in the dirt. Mima was alone, wasn't she? No family, nobody to go back to at the end of *Raku Nau*.

When she looked back up, Mima was lost in the flames all over again, not paying Jane any attention at all.

"And I think I understand her, too," Jane said.

Then she reached out and used her finger to draw a circle around all of them, together. Just like they were one team. Or a tribe.

Or a family.

Buzz felt an arm shaking him awake.

"Your turn," Carter whispered, and nudged him toward the fire. "I left you some more coconut if you want it."

Buzz sat up and shook the sleep out of his head. It was going to be another long day coming up. The sky was still dark, but he was the last one to take a watch, which meant he'd be up until sunrise. Mima, Jane, and Vanessa were sleeping spooned up together on the raft. Carter quickly lay down and was snoring within a few minutes.

Around the shore, Buzz could see the light of other fires. The only person he could actually see from where he sat was one of the boys in Chizo's group. His face was washed clean now—no more red and black—but just the way he kept staring across the distance was enough to creep Buzz out. There were no rules here, which meant that anything could happen at any time. It made sense for one of them to be awake to keep watch.

He glanced over at his siblings again, jealous that

they were all asleep. Even Mima had finally dropped off.

Just like on Nowhere Island, the long dark nights were the loneliest and the hardest part of surviving with nothing. The trek they had waiting for them in the morning wasn't going to be easy, but sitting alone through the night was the worst.

He picked up a rock Carter had chipped down to a sharp edge, and used it to whittle away at the new fishing spear Vanessa had started. Its point was already good and sharp, but Buzz kept working on it. At least it was a way to pass the time—and to distract his mind.

Hopefully, the sun would be coming up soon.

"Ba-nessa! Car-tare! Jane!"

Vanessa jerked awake. The sun hadn't risen yet, and the bay was cloaked in the gray gloom of predawn.

"What's going on?" Carter asked, sitting up.

Mima was standing over them. In fact, it was Mima who had shaken them awake, Vanessa realized. She'd slept so deeply it was hard to get her own thoughts straight. Now, Mima was speaking rapidly in Nukula and shooing them off the raft.

And as Vanessa looked around, she started to see why.

There were no fires burning up and down the shore anymore. Dozens of palm frond mats sat empty on the ground along the edge of the woods.

"Where is everyone?" Jane said.

"I think we overslept!" Vanessa said. "They're all gone!"

"Hang on—where's Buzz?" Carter asked.

They all fell into a silence, except for Mima. She'd begun dragging the raft toward the water. It seemed as though she wasn't going to wait for anyone—she was ready to start catching up to the others.

"Mima, we have to wait for Buzz!" Jane said to her. "Please!"

But Mima kept pointing toward the bay and pulling the raft on her own.

"Buzz!" Vanessa shouted.

"Buzz, come on!" Carter yelled. "We have to go!"

When Buzz didn't answer, it put a sinking feeling

in Vanessa's stomach. Maybe he had slipped off to go to the bathroom, but he wouldn't have been out of earshot. Would he?

Something was wrong. Very wrong.

"Carter?" she said. The words didn't even want to come out of her mouth. "I don't . . . think he's here anymore."

"I know," Carter answered grimly.

"Buzz!" Mima was calling from the water's edge. "Buzz!"

Vanessa whipped her head around, thinking Mima had just spotted him. Instead, she was pointing across the empty bay, toward Cloud Ridge in the distance.

It was like something clicked in that moment. Memories of their arrival on the island came flooding back—the way Carter had been ambushed, and how Jane had been taken in the woods. The deep pit in the sand. It had seemed like a big game for the Nukula at the time.

But it hadn't been a game, had it? It had been practice for *Raku Nau*, Vanessa realized.

Vanessa looked at Carter, then Jane, and they all seemed to know it at once.

"They took Buzz, didn't they?" Jane asked. Her voice cracked, and her eyes filled with tears.

"Yeah," Vanessa said. She scanned the area for any sign of which way they'd gone. It was hard to concentrate. Too many thoughts flew through her mind even to know what to do first.

"What does this mean?" Carter asked. "What are they going to do to him?"

"I don't know!" Vanessa said.

She thought again about what Ani had said the day before—*By any means necessary* . That wasn't just about winning a raft for crossing the bay, was it? It applied to all of *Raku Nau*. And if there were no rules, it meant Buzz could be anywhere by now. They had to do whatever they could to find him.

Maybe that also meant losing their chance of getting off the island, but it couldn't be helped. Not anymore. All that mattered was finding their brother.

By any means necessary.

EPILOGUE

Buzz trudged through the mud as the sun came up. His wrists were tied, and the vine they'd used to bind him extended ahead into Chizo's hand.

Chizo looked back. His face was re-painted, this time with green clay. When he smiled his white teeth stood out like a manic grimace.

"Where are you taking me?" Buzz asked for the tenth time. He didn't expect an answer, and he didn't get one.

"Chizo!" he said. "I'm talking to you!"

The boys seemed surprised Buzz knew his name. They stopped then and looked back at him. Chizo walked up close.

"Ah-ka-ah," he said. *"Chizo tetaka ekka-ko."*

"Whatever," Buzz said.

The strange part was, he knew he should be terrified. But something else had occurred to him after the capture.

"You're afraid of us, aren't you?" he said. "You didn't think we could beat you at anything, but we did. *We* won the raft. Not you!"

Maybe now he and his team were more of a threat than anyone had imagined they could be. And maybe *that* was why they'd taken him.

So, fine. If capture was part of *Raku Nau*, then so was escape. One way or another, Buzz thought, he wasn't going to let them just get away with this. He didn't know how, or where, or when—but this wasn't the end of the road for them.

They still had a long way to go.

The story continues in

STRANDED

SHADOW ISLAND

BOOK 2: **THE SABOTAGE**

Coming soon!

How much would you sacrifice? How far would you go? When Carter, Vanessa, Buzz, and Jane found themselves stranded on Shadow Island, they had no idea what they were getting into. Now one of their group is missing, and the stakes keep getting higher.

READ HOW THE ADVENTURE BEGAN IN

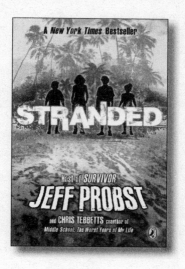

It was supposed to be a vacation—and a chance to get to know one another better. But when a massive storm sets in without warning, four kids are shipwrecked alone on a rocky jungle island in the middle of the South Pacific. No adults. No instructions. Nobody to rely on but themselves. Can they make it home alive?

A week ago, the biggest challenge Vanessa, Buzz, Carter, and Jane had was learning to live as a new blended family. Now the four siblings must find a way to work together if they're going to make it off the island. But first they've got to learn to survive one another.

It was day four at sea, and as far as eleven-year-old Carter Benson was concerned, life didn't get any better than this.

From where he hung, suspended fifty feet over the deck of the *Lucky Star*, all he could see was a planet's worth of blue water. The boat's huge white mainsail ballooned in front of him, filled with a stiff southerly wind that sent them scudding through the South Pacific faster than they'd sailed all week.

This was the best part of the best thing Carter had ever done, no question. It was like sailing and flying at the same time. The harness around his middle held him in place while his arms and legs hung free. The air itself seemed to carry him along, at speed with the boat.

"How you doin' up there, Carter?" Uncle Dexter shouted from the cockpit.

Carter flashed a thumbs-up and pumped his fist. "Faster!" he shouted back. Even with the wind whipping in his ears, Dex's huge belly laugh came back, loud and clear.

Meanwhile, Carter had a job to do. He wound the safety line from his harness in a figure eight around the cleat on the mast to secure himself. Then he reached over and unscrewed the navigation lamp he'd come up here to replace.

As soon as he'd pocketed the old lamp in his rain slicker, he pulled out the new one and fitted it into the fixture, making sure not to let go before he'd tightened it down. Carter had changed plenty of lightbulbs before, but never like this. If anything, it was all too easy and over too fast.

When he was done, he unwound his safety line and gave a hand signal to Dex's first mate, Joe

Kahali, down below. Joe put both hands on the winch at the base of the mast and started cranking Carter back down to the deck.

"Good job, Carter," Joe said, slapping him on the back as he got there. Carter swelled with pride and adrenaline. Normally, replacing the bulb would have been Joe's job, but Dex trusted him to take care of it.

Now Joe jerked a thumb over his shoulder. "Your uncle wants to talk to you," he said.

Carter stepped out of the harness and stowed it in its locker, just like Dex and Joe had trained him to do. Once that was done, he clipped the D-ring on his life jacket to the safety cable that ran the length of the deck and headed toward the back.

It wasn't easy to keep his footing as the *Lucky Star* pitched and rolled over the waves, but even that was part of the fun. If he did fall, the safety cable—also called a jackline—would keep him from going overboard. Everyone was required to stay clipped in when they were on deck, whether they were up there to work . . . or to puke, like Buzz was doing right now.

"Gross! Watch out, Buzz!" Carter said, pushing past him.

"*Uhhhhhnnnnh*," was all Buzz said in return. He was leaning against the rail and looked both green and gray at the same time.

Carter kind of felt sorry for him. They were both eleven years old, but they didn't really have anything else in common. It was like they were having two different vacations out here.

"Gotta keep moving," he said, and continued on toward the back, where Dex was waiting.

"Hey, buddy, it's getting a little choppier than I'd like," Dex said as Carter stepped down into the cockpit. "I need you guys to get below."

"I don't want to go below," Carter said. "Dex, I can help. Let me steer!"

"No way," Dex said. "Not in this wind. You've been great, Carter, but I promised your mom before we set sail—no kids on deck if these swells got over six feet. You see that?" He pointed to the front of the boat, where a cloud of sea spray had just broken over the bow. "*That's* what a six-foot swell looks like. We've got a storm on the way—maybe a big one. It's time for you to take a break."

"Come on, please?" Carter said. "I thought we came out here to sail!"

Dex took him by the shoulders and looked him square in the eye.

"Remember what we talked about before we set out? My boat. My rules. Got it?"

Carter got it, all right. Arguing with Dex was like wrestling a bear. You could try, but you were never going to win.

"Now, grab your brother and get down there," Dex told him.

"Okay, fine," Carter said. "But he's not my brother, by the way. Just because my mom married his dad doesn't mean—"

"Ask me tomorrow if I care," Dexter said, and gave him a friendly but insistent shove. "Now go!"

Benjamin "Buzz" Diaz lifted his head from the rail

and looked out into the distance. All he could see from here was an endless stretch of gray clouds over an endless stretch of choppy waves.

Keeping an eye on the horizon was supposed to help with the seasickness, but so far, all it had done was remind him that he was in the middle of the biggest stretch of nowhere he'd ever seen. His stomach felt like it had been turned upside down and inside out. His legs were like rubber bands, and his head swam with a thick, fuzzy feeling, while the boat rocked and rocked and rocked.

It didn't look like this weather was going to be changing anytime soon, either. At least, not for the better.

Buzz tried to think about something else—anything else—to take his mind off how miserable he felt. He thought about his room back home. He thought about how much he couldn't wait to get there, where he could just close his door and hang out all day if he wanted, playing City of Doom and eating pepperoni pizz—

Wait, Buzz thought. *No. Not that.*

He tried to unthink anything to do with food, but it was too late. Already, he was leaning over the rail again and hurling the last of his breakfast into the ocean.

"Still feeding the fish, huh?" Suddenly, Carter was back. He put a hand on Buzz's arm. "Come on," he said. "Dex told me we have to get below."

Buzz clutched his belly. "Are you kidding?" he said. "Can't it wait?"

"No. Come on."

All week long, Carter had been running around the deck of the *Lucky Star* like he owned it or something. Still, Carter was the least of Buzz's worries right now.

It was only day four at sea, and if things kept going like this, he was going to be lucky to make it to day five.

Vanessa Diaz sat at the *Lucky Star*'s navigation station belowdecks and stared at the laptop screen in front of her. She'd only just started to learn about this stuff a few days earlier, but as far as she could tell, all that orange and red on the weather radar was a bad sign. Not to mention the scroll across the bottom of the screen, saying something about "gale-force winds and deteriorating conditions."

The first three days of their trip had been nothing but clear blue skies and warm breezes. Now, nine hundred miles off the coast of Hawaii, all of that had changed. Dexter kept saying they had to adjust their course to outrun the weather, but so far, it seemed like the weather was outrunning them. They'd changed direction at least three times, and things only seemed to be getting worse.

The question was—how *much* worse?

A chill ran down Vanessa's spine as the hatch over the galley stairs opened, and Buzz and Carter came clattering down the steps.

"How are you feeling, Buzzy?" she asked, but he didn't stop to talk. Instead, he went straight for the little bathroom—the "head," Dexter called it—and slammed the door behind him.

Her little brother was getting the worst of these bad seas, by far. Carter, on the other hand, seemed unfazed.

Sometimes Vanessa called them "the twins," as a joke, because they were both eleven but nothing alike. Carter kept his sandy hair cut short and was even kind of muscley for a kid his age. Buzz, on the other hand, had shaggy jet-black curls like their father's and was what adults liked to call husky. The kids at school just called him fat.

Vanessa didn't think her brother was fat—not exactly—but you could definitely tell he spent a lot of time in front of the TV.

"It's starting to rain," Carter said, looking up at the sky.

"Then close the hatch," Vanessa said.

"Don't tell me what to do."

Vanessa rolled her eyes. "Okay, fine. Get wet. See if I care."

He would, too, she thought. He'd just stand there and get rained on, only because she told him not to. Carter was one part bulldog and one part mule.

Jane was there now, too. She'd just come out of the tiny sleeping cabin the two girls shared.

Jane was like the opposite of Carter. She could slip in and out of a room without anyone ever noticing. With Carter, you always knew he was there.

"What are you looking at, Nessa?" Jane asked.

"Nothing." Vanessa flipped the laptop closed. "I was just checking the weather," she said.

There was no reason to scare Jane about all that. She was only nine, and tiny for her age. Vanessa was the oldest, at thirteen, and even though nobody told her to look out for Jane on this trip, she did anyway.

"Dex said there's a storm coming," Carter blurted out. "He said it's going to be major."

"Carter!" Vanessa looked over at him and rolled her eyes in Jane's direction.

But he just shrugged. "What?" he said. "You think she's not going to find out?"

"You don't have to worry about me," Jane said.

She crawled up onto Vanessa's lap and opened the computer to have a look. "Show me."

"See?" Carter said. "I know my sister."

Vanessa took a deep breath. If the idea of this trip was to make them one big happy family, it wasn't exactly working.

Technically, the whole sailing adventure was a wedding gift from her new uncle, Dexter. It had been two months since Vanessa and Buzz's father had married Carter and Jane's mother, but they'd waited until the end of the school year to take a honeymoon. Now, while their parents were hiking Volcanoes National Park and enjoying the beaches on Hawaii's Big Island, the four kids were spending the week at sea and supposedly getting to know one another better.

So far, the sailing had been amazing, but the sister-brother bonding thing? Not so much, Vanessa thought. The weather wasn't helping, either. It looked like they were going to be cooped up together for the rest of the day.

"Is that the storm?" Jane said. She pointed at the large red mass on the laptop screen.

"That's it," Vanessa answered. On the computer, it seemed as if the oncoming front had gotten even bigger in the last few minutes. She started braiding Jane's long blond hair to distract her.

"It's just rain, right?" Jane said. "If this was something really bad, we'd already know about it. Wouldn't we, Nessa?"

Vanessa tried to smile. "Sure," she said. But the truth was, she had no idea how bad it was going to get.

None of them did.

THE ADVENTURE CONTINUES IN

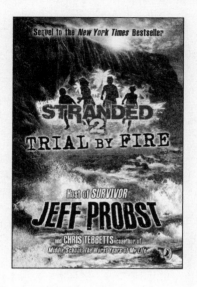

They thought it couldn't get any worse. They were wrong. Being shipwrecked on a jungle island was bad enough. But now that Carter, Vanessa, Buzz, and Jane have lost their boat to another storm, it's like starting over. Survival is no individual sport in a place like this, but there's only one way to learn that. The hard way.

LOOK FOR BOOK THREE!

It's been days since Buzz, Vanessa, Carter, and Jane were stranded in the middle of the South Pacific. No adults. No supplies. Nothing but themselves and the jungle. And they've lost their only shelter, and quite possibly their one chance at being rescued. Now they must delve even deeper into Nowhere Island for food and supplies. But the island has a few secrets of its own to tell. . . . With danger at every turn, this blended family has to learn how to trust one another if they stand any chance of survival.